Thunder and
beneath the sea...

The murky galleys were choked with eye-burning
smog.

One son of Hades had taken the full brunt of the
explosion and lay sprawled on the deck, his body a
sack of broken bones.

A second Jeddah killer stood in blind confusion,
low gibberish pouring from his cherry-red mouth.

A third terrorist had been hurled horizontally by the
concussion into a gaping torpedo tube. His body
was jammed into the hole headfirst all the way to
the elbows. His feet kicked feebly as the suffocating
tube sucked the life from him.

"All okay here," Gary Manning called. "They're all
taken care of!"

PHOENIX FORCE

AN EXECUTIONER SERIES

Atlantic Scramble

Don Pendleton & Gar Wilson

A GOLD EAGLE BOOK FROM

WORLDWIDE

TORONTO · NEW YORK · LOS ANGELES · LONDON

First edition November 1982

ISBN 0-373-61303-2

Special thanks and acknowledgement to Thomas Ramirez
for his contributions to this work.

Printed in Canada

This book is dedicated to those poor suffering bastards who somehow are still idealistic enough to summon up the courage to blow the whistle on government stupidity and rapacious politicians. The battle goes on, today, tomorrow, but, one hopes, not forever. One day soon, America will regain the pride promised in its birthing rituals.

Katz—a French-Israeli intelligence veteran with one arm. Unbeatable in combat.

Gary Manning—a Canadian explosives engineer. Incredibly strong, he thrives on trouble.

Keio Ohara—a Japanese master of martial arts. Unusually tall. Unusually deadly.

David McCarter—a British brawler, famous for his SAS activities. Rude. Rugged. Ruthless.

Rafael Encizo—a Cuban survivor of Castro's prisons, expert in underwater warfare. Altogether fearless.

Phoenix Force is Mack Bolan's five-man army that fights the dirtiest of wars. They trust, respect and care deeply for each other, bonded by the extremes of their combat experiences. They are all-action.

PROLOGUE

It was high noon, a crisp, warm, Indian summer day in the gritty heart of New York City, when Colonel Yakov Katzenelenbogen—Phoenix Force's nominal commander—received his summons. Inside the Museum of Modern Art he and his stunning female companion stood before van Gogh's *Starry Night*.

And while the tall, distinguished man with the receding hairline made sweeping gestures with his ivory cane (his right hand gloved to conceal his artificial hand, souvenir of the loss of his forearm during the Six Day War in 1967) while he extolled the texture and intensity of the artist's primitive invention, his companion's mind drifted.

Madame Solange Michaud, wife of a prominent French UN diplomat, thought instead of the impending luncheon with Katz at the Four Seasons. More importantly, she anticipated the passionate interlude they would share at her apartment later that afternoon. She knew very well that Yakov's ardor for art, literature and philosophy washed over into things physical as well. She shivered erotically, thought perhaps to skip lunch.

Now, as Katzenelenbogen explained his addiction to *Starry Night*, its visitation a matter of near-holy pilgrimage whenever he hit New York—a recharging of his soul—she saw him start suddenly, make vague pass at the hearing-aid button in his left ear. His words died. He seemed to be listening to far-off voices.

"If you'll excuse me, darling," he said urgently, his eyes suddenly bright with a new light, "I forgot an important phone call." He escorted her up a flight of stairs, seated her on an upholstered bench. "Please wait here. I'll be right back." Then he walked away purposefully, looking somehow taller, more powerful all at once, despite the slight limp and the ever-present cane.

Solange's heart fell when he returned, for she read the expression on his face. Resolution tinged with deep regret. "Oh, Yakov," she wailed softly, "not again. We have so few moments together."

"Something's come up, my dear," he said in his clipped accent. "I'm afraid I must beg you to excuse me. A very necessary bit of business I must tend to immediately."

"Right this minute?" She colored slightly. "Surely you can delay for an hour. If we were to...." She dropped her gaze. "I mean...go directly...."

He leaned close, touched her lovely lips with a tenderness that made her ache. "If only it could be, my love. I die inside also. But it is an extremely crucial matter." He took her arm firmly, lifted her. "I'll get you a cab."

They kissed briefly at the curb, the touch of her wet, soft lips, the exotic fragrance of her perfume causing him to waver for the briefest moment. "I'll make it up to you. Soon. It will be heavenly, I swear...."

Solange smiled in resignation, tried to cling a second longer, but he stiffened and she took her cue. She looked up at him from the cab a last time. "Yakov, darling?"

"Yes?"

"That little thing in your ear. It's not *really* a hearing aid, is it?"

He sent her an enigmatic smile, made no answer. He was still standing, waving sadly after her, as the cab hit Fifth Avenue and turned right.

Jogging on a thickly wooded hiking trail winding through Canada's Mont Tremblant Park, Gary Manning sensed definite disquiet. His last contact with Stony Man had been ten days ago. He had been told the pursuit was getting hot, that definite standby was in effect. Which irritated Manning. Christ, he thought, shouldn't they have pinpointed the Jeddah strike by now?

Manning sucked in the cool, astringent air, savored the autumn panorama unfolding before him. Indian summer with a vengeance. How, he chafed, could any man in his right mind choose to live in a city when he could have this? He thought of Toronto, Quebec City, even Montreal, lovely as they were, and wondered how he'd abided them as long as he had. And now, St. Donat, some sixty-odd miles northwest of Montreal, where he had lived these past four years. God's country, and no mistake! The hunting, the fishing, the solitude—total escape from the reek of man.

Picking up his pace, Manning concentrated on a stand of oak trees ahead, rusty red, contrasted against an endless plain of dubloon yellow aspens. His smile broadened. He'd try for ten miles today.

Fifty-six minutes later Manning broke into the clearing where the day's jog had originally begun. Breathing hard, he made for the hidden dirt road where he had cached his powerful sports car. Stony Man still on his mind, he opened the door, switched on the high-powered CB radio that he had installed himself. He clicked to channel twenty-two, trusted that the answering-service lady would be monitoring as instructed every time he went running.

"Breaker twenty-two for Tess Trueheart. You've got the Blue Marlin here. Do you copy?"

"Tess Trueheart," the radio crackled shortly. "Go, Marlin."

"Any messages?"

"Yes, Blue Marlin. There's a call from a Mr. Rudolph Hess. He requests an immediate callback."

"Ten-forty. I'll be heading in right away."

Manning dropped the mike into its slot and stepped out of the car. The call at last. Ominous dread came down suddenly. This was the one he had been waiting on so long. He began walking in wide circles to cool down. Gradually his breathing evened out; the sweat began to dry on his body.

Again he stared down into the autumn caldron of color, was hit by a mixture of emotions: elation intermixed with impatience, plus a sizable quotient of fear.

Time, Gary. His heart revved even harder as the call's full impact hit home. It's finally got to be that time. Sense of impending disaster grew. It could be time, after all, to die.

He turned his morbid thoughts off and returned to the car.

The Ferrari 308GTS was without exception the only real indulgence allowed in Manning's pragmatic, stripped-down life-style. A mild sense of loss came to him as he jammed himself behind the wheel. How long—if ever—before I goose this little bomb to life again?

The engine fired, roared, purred, docile yet tough. Expertly he ran the gears, knew a feeling akin to lust as the low-slung racer hit concrete, hunkered down, ready for business. He accelerated smoothly, and the GTS leaped out like a fuck-starved jackrabbit. And though the highway back to St. Donat had apparently been laid out by a drunken snake, Manning nevertheless pushed the Ferrari at a steady eighty all the way back.

In the cool apartment located in the heart of Miami's Little Havana there came the unexpected—and unwanted—interruption.

"Por favor, amado," pleaded an exquisite tawnyskinned female, wearing nothing but a smiling promise of passion eternal. "Don't answer it." She clung fiercely, arching her leg over Rafael to keep him beside her. "Every damned time things get a little bit interesting around here," she complained, her accent the slightest bit chili-kissed, "that phone has to ring."

"Callate, muñeca," Rafael Encizo muttered as he gently unpeeled her from his chest and hips, evading her coaxing kisses. "I *have* to answer. There's something big hanging fire. This could be the call I'm waiting on."

"You and your big deals," Teresa grumbled. "Every time you get one of those calls I don't see you for a month."

Rafael strode into the living room and picked up the receiver. "Encizo," he said, his voice low so the pouting Teresa could not hear. He picked up electronic babble in the earpiece. He knew instantly this was no wrong number. He punched buttons on a desk control and took up the scrambler receiver. "Repeat message from the top," he snapped.

His pulse was racing. Moonlight on the killing ground, he exulted...and about time too. Rusting of the blood was a constant worry to Encizo.

He took no incriminating notes of Katzenelenbogen's staccato instructions; practice over the years enabled him to commit yards of error-free information to memory. "I'll get the first flight out. El Paso, right. Holiday Inn? How prosaic. Check." And with subdued affection: "I'm looking forward to working with you again, *compadre*."

Teresa teased him as he returned to the bedroom. "When do you leave?" she said, her tongue provocatively lubricating her lips.

"Yesterday," Encizo said, standing in naked distraction, trying to marshall his thoughts. The brute stereo rig—H.H. Scott integrated amplifier pushing one hundred fifty watts per channel—played soft mood music into the bedroom speakers.

She came into his arms as he fell beside her on the bed. "Oh, darling," she choked, "if you only knew how much I worry about you. You always come back all chewed up and tired, your eyes haunted, like you've been to hell and back...."

"Corazón," he muttered soothingly, "I always come back. I always find ways to make it up to you, to make you happy, don't I?"

He held her more tightly, his heart filling up. He breathed in the scent of her hair, of her body, and thought that he must someday quit running from the past. He must someday make a commitment to a woman again. Why not Teresa? She loved him. The thrust of her charming and provocative breasts, the tight yet voluptuous mounds of her ass caused his gut to twist. He was sure he loved her, as much as he could ever love any woman again.

But always there came the mocking specter of Estella Maria, of her bomb-mangled body, of the uncomprehending expression on what had remained of her face. His wife—victim of a pro-Castro faction. Could he again expose another woman to that kind of treachery and danger? Could he bear that pain, survive that deranging fury? It had been a rage that caused Rafael Encizo to dedicate his life totally to vendetta against terrorist thugs. It was a rage that had eventually brought him to Stony Man, to Mack Bolan—to Colonel John Phoenix, the new Executioner.

And to Katzenelenbogen, to McCarter, to Ohara, to Manning.

To Phoenix Force.

"I'll come back, *querida*," he assured fervently, "I'll always come back. The man has not been born yet who can put *me* away."

In Alameda, California it was 10:15 A.M., and after a ninety-minute session of Nautilus drills at Muscle City, Keio Ohara was back in his Alameda Street apartment. Clad in a flowing robe, otherwise naked, sitting cross-legged on a straw mat before a matted Kunisada print (one of the few frills in his Spartan surroundings), he meditated.

Having achieved the second plane of inner detachment, shutting out street noises that carried from three stories below, he now strove to attain the third phase, where he would float free in mystic limbo. But where normally the desired state of nirvana came with relative case, today he could not push himself across the amorphous barrier. He could blot out the world—the planes coming across San Francisco Bay, the boats tootling warning in the cold drizzle and fog—but the turmoil in his soul, niggling phantom of the impending Phoenix Force mission, could not be dispelled.

Ohara's desperation grew, and he concentrated harder on the antique Japanese print, a gnarled cypress clinging to the face of a craggy cliff, as if seeking to enter the scene itself and feel the cold mountain wind on his face, smell the pungent pine needles. He drew on all the teachings to help block worldly thoughts. He would be spiritual today, he would lay up reserves of strength and confidence for the superhuman challenge facing him. His life and the lives of his comrades would depend upon it.

The man who sat thus in his sparsely furnished room was tall and rangy, unusual for an Oriental. His face—thin, angular—also belied his ancestry, his black eyes not quite as heavily lidded as those of the average Japanese, his complexion tending more to a healthy tanned tone than the regulation sallowness.

Because of his long legs (Keio was six feet tall) his

walk was somewhat ungainly, but when he ran his movements were fluid, tiger swift, reminiscent of O.J. Simpson in his heyday.

Polite and soft spoken, he had the aura of a pussycat. Too bad for anyone who chose to take advantage, for he would soon find himself scraping his body off the sidewalk. Keio was skilled in judo and kendo, and was holder of a black belt in karate. He trained twice weekly with an advanced class in Oakland, and entered competitions compulsively.

Dynamite always comes in a plain brown wrapper.

Ohara's dark brows became furrowed as he took deep, even breaths, fighting for the evasive tranquillity that would replenish his soul. But it seemed hopeless, for the doubts were back; again he questioned his usefulness to Phoenix Force.

At twenty-eight, the youngest man on the team, he had the least amount of actual combat experience. How could he ever begin to compare with Katz and his Mossad background, his blooding in the Six Day War? Or with Encizo, who had fought at the Bay of Pigs, had singlehandedly escaped from Castro's hellhole Principe Prison? And McCarter, with his Laos-Vietnam mileage, and his participation in the SAS storming of the Iranian Embassy in London in 1980?

He sighed heavily. One of these days he'd make a bad decision, or his reaction time would be a millisecond slow, and one of his friends would die for his mistake. Would it not be best if he had a serious talk with Katz? While there was still time to recruit a replacement before Phoenix pushed off on its next mission?

But suddenly there was no more time for destructive self-evaluation; nor would Ohara attain that third plane of detachment. The phone jangled. Even as he rose from the mat he knew that the nervous anticipation was over. He engaged the scrambler line before he lifted the receiver.

He felt an overpowering desire and excitement. Keio *wanted* to go, he wanted to battle shoulder-to-shoulder with his friends once again! He yearned for one real chance to prove himself, to be counted among the ranks of this elite force—to be recognized over and over as one of the toughest bastards on the face of the earth.

David McCarter's summons reached him in Las Vegas. It was 9:45 A.M., and still eternal night in his semi-deserted corner of Caesar's Palace. McCarter was coming off an all-night stint at the blackjack tables. He was definitely spaced out, in no shape for dragon slaying at the moment.

He had been gambling since midnight. Somewhere in that long, liquor-muddled evening he had joined forces with an eager little playmate, a vacationing secretary, cute and cuddly, who had had definite designs on how the night should end. And why not? What better way to kill time? That had been David's main reason for checking out Las Vegas in the first place. If Stony Man was putting him on hold anyway, what more exciting place to hole up?

There had been dinner at the MGM, then on to the Stardust and its Lido de Paris extravaganza. As the scads of luscious nude bodies had got to them there had been kisses, heavy breathing, fleeting lap work. She became the original sure thing.

How they got to Caesar's, and into blackjack, he could not really recall. He had corrected small errors in her strategy and then Debby had done well, running her stake to three hundred dollars. At which point the little dear got greedy for other things. It was time to play house. The nagging started. "Please, Davey? Can't we go now? It's getting so late...."

But Davey was down six hundred bucks, and he wasn't about to fold just then. He gave Debby a couple of chips and sent her to play the slots; he'd only be a half hour or so. But then he had gotten hot, could seemingly do no wrong. By the time she returned he was two thousand ahead. And did the dumbbell actually think he was going to cash in when he was on a roll?

Snit time then. "Call me later, David," she snapped as she flounced off, "when you come to your senses. Seems to me a real man would have a more mature sense of priorities."

"Stupid cow," he grumbled when she was gone. And to the smirking dealer: "There'll be another. Easy come, easy go."

Angry, a bit torn, he upped his bet to five hundred. At which the dealer had accommodatingly dealt him two aces. McCarter immediately split, pushed forward five more chips. The dealer dealt two face cards, and David was suddenly one thousand five richer. He'd almost chortled out loud. It was going to be one of those nights! No nooky ever could beat this for fun, right, mate?

Right.

So the night had slipped away from him, his streak taking him as high as twelve thousand by 6:00 A.M. But from then on it mostly downhill. At 7:00 he'd been down to ten, seven five at 8:00. By 8:30 there was modest comeback, and he'd climbed to nine.

At this moment McCarter was staring groggily at a pot of six thousand three. He was drained, could hardly concentrate. It wasn't money anymore, just a mass of multicolored chips signifying the player's innate game-smarts, his luck—or pure stupidity. And why didn't he just chuck it for now, cash in? Las Vegas would stay open.

Hopeless stubbornness prevailed, and he saw the pot shrink to three, then two thousand. He dazedly pushed out another two fifty. Two thousand five. It was the way of the modern English. Keep muddling through.

McCarter's pager made one dulcet beep. He jerked, came halfway alert, hoisted it from its holster, flipped the switch. "McCarter," he said blearily.

"A Mr. Rudolph Hess just called," the crisp voice said. "He requests an immediate callback."

McCarter put the pager away. Fleeting thoughts of Debby—an opportunity missed forever—struck him momentarily. Sorry, darling. The breaks. Someone else gets to be *numero uno*.

He regarded the dealer dourly, shoved all his chips forward with a decisive move. "Sir..." the dealer protested.

"Ask the man," David snapped, indicating the pit boss.

After hurried conference, the dealer came back. "He says okay."

It was head-to-head with the house. The cards slid from the shoe. David held an eight and a seven. Dealer showed a queen. He took a deep breath, whisked for a hit.

His heart leaped as the five showed. He covered his cards, sat on twenty.

The dealer turned over his down card. Queen four.

McCarter's breath froze as the dealer's third card hissed across the green felt. Seven. A perfect twenty-one.

McCarter could hear his heart explode.

The dealer's face was expressionless as he raked in the pile of chips. McCarter showed a thin grin. He maintained a slow, cocky swagger as he walked from the table. "Easy come, easy go," he called back over his shoulder.

The dealer didn't even bother to look up.

1

Crazy things were happening at Red Bluff Arsenal, things nobody could explain. Total shutdown—swift, unexpected—had come at 1500 hours. All civilians and GIs living off-post were allowed a single phone call to alert family members and that was it. Temporary security alert was the only explanation given to the hundred-seventy-two-man complement: orders from Corps, presumably relayed from the Pentagon.

All passes into Odessa, Texas, located eighteen miles southeast of the low-profile experimental installation, were immediately canceled. All outlying logistical personnel were recalled.

The camp was locked tight, completely isolated from the world.

Why, nobody knew.

The afternoon was muggy, overcast, and the troops were confined to quarters while civilian technicians huddled in offices and labs until chow time. Topkicks could pry no fresh poop from the C.O.; the C.O. could get nothing from headquarters. Colonel Ballard was locked in his office, no calls going in or coming out. In fact, neither Ballard nor any of his staff officers had been seen since noon.

Stranger and stranger.

Later a chill rain had begun to fall, and most of the personnel donned rain gear when mess call sounded at 1700 hours. The civilians, assigned makeshift billeting in an unused barracks, ate in one corner of the officers' mess. Like the enlisted men, they faced conventional army fare, overcooked beef tenderloin, runny mashed potatoes, peas, tasteless bread, chalky ice cream.

Things became more curious still as night fell. Now there were unexpected changes of the guard, of duty officers. A high-strung, belligerent cadre of noncoms checked barracks, latrines, day rooms and orderly rooms for malingerers, herded them into the mess hall, saw to it that everyone got fed.

Then the complaints started:

"Holy Christ, Bob, what's with that chow we had tonight?" T-4 Chuck Staniske asked of his bunk-mate. "Tasted okay when I ate it, but now I'm so thirsty I could die. Haven't stopped drinking water since supper. Put down two quarts, I'll bet."

"Same here," replied PFC Robert Markert. "And, man, I feel so damned sluggish, like someone just zapped me. Look at my hand—I can hardly move it. My legs feel like they're asleep or something. What'n hell time is it, anyway?"

At which Staniske fought to raise his right wrist, groaned wearily as he accomplished it. "Only seven-thirty. Shit, I thought it was midnight, at least. I'm gonna crash. Talk about being zonked...."

The eerie transformation of healthy, strong men into closed-down zombies was occurring all over Red Bluff Arsenal—in the four enlisted men's barracks, in the quarters occupied by the civilians and the officers as well. By 2000 hours the entire camp was asleep. No sounds heard, no movements to be seen. Street traffic ceased. There was only the steady drumming of the rain. The installation was wrapped in a shroud.

But one last holdout, Corporal John Bluewing, a Navaho Indian possessed of a cast-iron stomach, was still abroad. He had stumbled from the latrine and tried to make his way to his barracks. He fought to make every step, then laughed with soft bemusement as he collapsed on his ass in a puddle. "Well, I'll be a blue-assed monkey," he muttered, his voice a deep bass.

A figure melted from the blackness, came toward John Bluewing. "Hey, buddy," the man said—he was wearing fatigues and a helmet liner, and he had an accent—"having troubles?" He came behind Bluewing, gruntingly lifted him, began guiding him toward the nearest barracks. "Too much to drink, huh?"

"No drink," the corporal muttered thickly. "Jus' so tired. . . ." He looked up at his rescuer, fought to focus his vision. "Hey, you're new. I never saw you around here before. . . ."

The helpful GI did not answer. Certainly exhibiting no signs of weakness himself, he got John up the stoop and wedged open the barracks' door. Viciously he pushed his burden inside, enjoying the crunch of his body as the Indian hit the floor, sprawled helplessly. "Good enough, Jack," came the alien voice. "You keep right there."

The door slammed and he was gone, his feet clattering on the boardwalk. Inside the barracks no one was heard, no one made a move to help the groaning man on the floor.

Perhaps an hour later, all barracks dark, a dozen or so men carried flashlights and made one last hurried bedcheck, searched various orderly rooms to ensure that the infiltration was complete. At the guard shacks at the main entrance, a new breed of MPs— lean and slight of stature—now took charge. At CP the switchboard still lit up sporadically, and again and again the dark-skinned male operator answered in sing-song accent, "Sorry, I have orders to put no calls through." Polite but firm.

So the strange night went on, menace growing. Red Bluff was out of touch with the world, adrift and floating in a deep sea of night. "Sorry, I have orders to...."

First Lieutenant Ramos had been assigned to Red Bluff Arsenal perhaps two months earlier as replacement to Colonel Ballard's retiring adjutant. His records impeccable, his manner forthright, yet somehow self-deprecating, he had quickly ingratiated himself with the colonel. Ballard particularly enjoyed his broad-minded approach to things ethnic. In a state where bean jokes were national humor, Ramos, a Mexican himself, could tell them with a real flair.

And why don't Mexicans like barbecues? the colonel asked his new adjutant. Because the beans keep falling through the grate....

Only tonight the joke was on Ballard. Now Lieutenant Ramos, seated beside the couch in Colonel Ballard's office—on which Ballard, at that moment, reclined in sullen torpor—was finally ready to reveal his true identity. As his assistant, again in green fatigues and helmet-liner, expertly injected a small syringe into the sleeping colonel's arm, Ramos smiled, and waited for this antidote to take effect.

Credit must certainly be given where credit was due, the darkly handsome lieutenant mused as he noted Ballard's first twitchings. Jeddah—and Khader Ghazawi—never did things halfway. Thus far their master scheme had worked flawlessly. The forged papers, the long train of counterfeit orders even now being cut. Magic passports that would carry them across America, across the Atlantic— back to Libya! The U.S. military bureaucracy, like its governmental one, had been such child's play. And if the rest of it went as well as this first phase had gone. . . .

Once Red Anvil delivered the super-advanced weaponry it would shortly liberate from Red Bluff, the signal for the holy war to commence would sound out loud. The Red Sea would truly run red! With Jewish blood! And he, Janda Yamani, alias Lieutenant Ramos, would sit at that bargaining table. Red Anvil would achieve power beyond Yamani's wildest dreams. Power would beget power. There was no telling what influence Red Anvil—and its courageous leader, Ghazawi—could attain once new empires were carved from the Middle East.

Abruptly the dark-skinned, treacherous, masquerading U.S. Army lieutenant set leash to his flamboyant reverie, to his unbridled fanaticism. First things first, he cautioned. Things like getting those guns loaded, delivering them to the initial rendezvous at the appointed time.

He slapped Ballard sharply across the face, jarring him back from the final edge of torpor. "Colonel Ballard! Do you know who I am?"

Ballard, revived by the antidote, stared dully at Yamani, but nothing registered in his eyes. "No."

"Do you know what is happening to you? To the whole camp?"

"No."

"Just as well. You would never forgive yourself if you did." The lieutenant turned to his accomplice. "Sarafid," he ordered, "we will need at least twenty strong men. See to it."

The man picked up a squat medical case and promptly headed into the night. In the darkness a jeep roared off.

"Colonal Ballard. Is Ben Harper still chief engineer in charge of the laser machine-gun testing?"

"Yes."

"Good. Let us go find him."

Where Ballard had been comatose moments before, he was now in a strange way restored. Save in one important respect: Though he could comprehend, speak and obey commands, he was still a zombie who no longer had any ability to refuse an order—no matter how contrary it might run to his training and standards.

They crossed the compound and entered the barracks housing the civilians. Yamani smiled as he saw the colonel's awkward gait, like a puppet reaching out for strings that were not there. In the gloom the moribund bodies about them resembled so many lifeless cadavers. The lights flashed on, the sudden glare stabbing Yamani's eyes. But neither Ballard nor the sleeping men even flinched. Harper was six bunks down the aisle. He was a balding, rotund man in his early fifties.

Yamani produced another small syringe, and sat beside the engineer and punched it into his arm. As he waited—with Ballard immobile, like an unwound toy, at the door—he said to the unhearing Harper, "You'd be interested in this, old man. A precise blending of thorazine and a newly discovered by-product of GB/Sarin—give thanks to our Russian friends—will bring you out of a twenty-four-hour comatose state and return you for a while to semi-intelligence. You will not remember any of this, ever. You'll never know that you lost a day out of your life."

Again the jolting slap on the cheek. "Come, Harper! We have work to do."

Ten seconds later, Harper's eyes fluttered open. The zombified test engineer fought his way up from the bed, sluggishly steadied his feet on the floor, his eyes all the while staring blankly into space.

In barracks two, Emida Sarafid, Yamani's second-in-command, was at that moment going from bed to bed, pulling up shirtsleeves, shooting two thousand milligrams of the antidote into each arm. The line of men stretched before him like so much cordwood, bodies suspended in grotesque time warp. Slowly, one by one, they spasmed, uttering small groans, awakening as if from a bad nightmare. They began sitting up.

Five minutes later Janda Yamani, trailed by Ballard and Harper, broke into the brightly lit barracks. "All right, men. Fall out! On the double!"

A robot platoon spilled onto the rain-puddled company street, formed ranks, dressed with arms right and came to attention. The only sound heard was the muffled shuffle of their boots. Otherwise the world had died. There was only a dull pewter streak on the horizon to announce birth of a new day.

Five ten-ton trucks, driven by Red Anvil cadre, were waiting at the fortified gate of the weapons depository where the parade of wooden soldiers arrived.

"Colonel Ballard," Yamani said, in a cordial manner as he escorted the colonel to a reinforced bunker that housed the computerized locking mechanism, "since you are the only man who has the combination to this thing...." Ballard robotically searched his pockets, then inserted three separate computer cards to trip the bunker locks. Once inside, he mechanically pressed a series of numbers into a Honeywell 1200 and the progression began. Forty-five seconds later the massive, fourteen feet wide, double-thick steel doors rolled aside. "Where are the Desslers stored?" Yamani insisted.

"Compartment fourteen," Ballard replied, his voice hollow.

"Sarafid! Move the trucks in. There are one thousand pieces in section fourteen. Take all available ammunition, replacement kits as well. Hurry. We have two hours to work."

Amidst the noise of echoing commands, Yamani, addressed Harper: "I'll need a quick briefing. Let's visit that fancy laboratory of yours. Ballard, you come too."

The long table was soon piled with reams of testing

reports, specification sheets, blueprints and manuals, all stamped TOP SECRET. There was no time to fully digest any of the materials, but Yamani demanded latest update, general guidance.

"The Dessler laser submachine gun," Harper began in listless monotone, "is aimed through use of a laser sight, and is foolproof, jamfree and one hundred percent accurate at ranges up to one thousand feet. It fires a .22-caliber explosive bullet, and is the most advanced and effective and ultimately useful anti-personnel weapon likely to be seen in the next ten years. The staggered magazine holds four hundred eighty-seven shells and is capable of total unload in...."

As the voice droned on, Yamani felt his excitement grow. Better and better, he gloated, even better than Ghazawi had led us to believe. Already he could visualize the explosive bullets as they impacted, blowing apart throngs of men, women and children, splattering gore on walls and sidewalks throughout the Promised Land. With a weapon like this there was no way on earth that Jeddah could fail.

He felt a craving to field-test this gun himself, to feel the kick and bite of the DLSG's stock against his shoulder, to hear its stuttering song of death. But not now. Later. Perhaps in the crowded streets of capital cities? Lieutenant Ramos, now and forever Janda Yamani, was a warrior of the devil, that destroyer from the underworld identified in every religion. He was the anti-life.

His guts churned from the visions of evil now overdosing his system.

A half hour later, while the world was bathed in

the eerie steel gray of dawn, Yamani, Harper and Ballard emerged from the lab, found half the trucks already loaded, the troops staggering under the bulky, unmarked crates, their steps robotlike at a pace that might not falter until doomsday.

Yeah, and that would be soon enough. But the troops made no complaint, showed no expression of weariness or discontent as box upon box disappeared into the yawning trucks.

"How's it going?" Yamani asked Sarafid.

"We are almost loaded. We will have one truck empty."

Yamani smiled sarcastically. "Hardly." And to Harper: "What else do you have in this marvelous gun shop of yours? What other new weapons we might look at?"

"The XM-ten-twenty-two," Harper replied in blithe babble. "It's a new mortar with a range of twelve thousand meters, farther than any existing mortar known. It carries a fragmentation charge laced with high-fuse thermite and aluminum-magnesium that will penetrate to six inches. The internal burns, almost a spontaneous combustion within the body, will prove one hundred percent fatal. In addition...."

"Enough," Yamani laughed. "That one sounds perfectly charming. We'll take all you've got. Come, Ballard. Let's go open the compartment."

Another fifty minutes passed before the fifth truck was crammed to capacity with two hundred and fifty state-of-the-art XM-1022 mortars, plus four thousand rounds of matching ammo. "Almost enough material to start a war for the history books," Emida

Sarafid announced with unnerving complacency. He and his captain watched the GIs secure the tailgates and snug down the tarpaulins.

"Indeed." Yamani was savoring the moment. He was filled with a bloating sense of victory. It had been so easy! If the mission continued in the same way, the shipment should be in Libya by week's end. These infidel Americans...so trusting. Their own powers worked against them the minute you infiltrated the bureaucracy, put fake forms and other well-aimed wrenches into the power machine. Perhaps, once we finish with the Jews....

He absorbed the thought, lashed out at Sarafid: "You are sure of the coordinates? Good. Then move out! I'll alert those who will remain behind. Ahmed and I will catch up in the Jeep. *Allah yesallimek*."

"Allah be with you, my brother captain."

Five minutes later the gates closed behind the convoy. When the gates opened again, a jeep sped against the clearing horizon to catch up with the lumbering death-laden caravan. Now they were at Gilchrist Highway, silhouetted against the sunsplashed escarpments of the Guadalupe Mountains. Heading due west, the convoy dipped into a swale, was seen no more.

At the CP, the rearguard faction continued to fight off the fresh intrusions of a workaday world. "We have orders to put no calls through," the weary operator repeated again and again.

At the main gate the dark-skinned MPs, talking politely but firmly about security alerts, fended off delivery people, a roof repair crew, two anxious wives wailing of emergencies at home.

While within Red Bluff Arsenal—

All was peaceful and silent. The world was put on hold. Those men still in their bunks grimaced at the bitter taste in their mouths, turned over, snuggled themselves deeper into a dreamless sleep.

2

It was shortly after nine when Colonel Yakov Katzenelenbogen, Keio Ohara flanking him in the front seat of the 1980 Buick Skylark, both of them dressed in civilian attire, drew up to the sentry post at Red Bluff Arsenal. Though they could not know it, they were already hours too late.

McCarter, Encizo and Manning waited in an IH four-wheel-drive Scout parked off the road two miles back, surrounded by mesquite, cactus, scrub pine, acres of rippled sand and gravel.

On constant CB monitor, they could respond to the slightest suggestion of a Mayday with the undivided precision of a hurtling wall. And would.

Even before the Buick rolled to full stop, the hook-nosed, mahogany-toned MP emerged from the guard hut. Beyond him loomed a six-foot-high cyclone fence, electrified most likely, and topped with six strands of barbed wire. Beyond that, parked crossways on the road itself—should anyone think of storming the Bastille—stood a ten-ton truck. "Sorry, gentlemen," the man said in a clear, cultured accent, standard .45 on his hip, "but the post is closed to all visitors today. We are observing an alert here."

Since when did GIs speak such impeccable BBC English? Katz brooded upon the unmistakable odor of rat, which he now detected.

"Alert? What sort of an alert?" Nothing was moving within the gates, not a soul was to be seen anywhere.

"Security alert, sir. Please move along."

"But I had an appointment with Colonel Ballard." Katz passed a phony business card to the guard. "We were going to discuss some modifications to his insurance policy. Nine-fifteen, he told me."

"No insurance," the guard intoned. "No nothing. The camp is closed until further notice. I have my orders. Now move along."

Inside Yak's jacket was holstered a .357 Combat Magnum. Inside Ohara's, a well-known Mack Bolan special, the .44 AutoMag pistol. At his feet, concealed by a car blanket, lay a compact submachine gun, the Ingram MAC-10, a permanent fixture in their portable arsenal. Back in the Scout were grenades, mortars, the CAR-15 that Manning especially favored, the Stoner M-63 A1 that was Encizo's old friend. And McCarter had his AK-47. And they were not dressed in anything approximating civilian attire.

"How long is this security alert in effect?" Katz persisted.

"Can't say. We do not have that information. Call administration later today. Now move, sir!"

Katz peered at the guard's coloration. Indian? Chicano? Italian? *"¿Habla usted español?"* he tested.

"I said move along. I will not be asking you again."

"Lei parla l'italiano?"

The MP angrily summoned a buddy from the other hut. His backup was also dark, hawk-nosed.

"A'rabee hone?" Katz screwed the Arabic zinger home. He exulted in the way both men's eyes clicked with his.

"You must leave now. The camp is closed. This is your last warning."

Katz slowly turned the car. Then he headed back on the road to Odessa. He smiled at Keio. "They're here," he said.

Phoenix Force had been fully gathered in El Paso, in rooms 224 and 226 of Holiday Inn West, by 2200 hours the previous night. McCarter, much strung out, had been the first to check in, Manning the last. But their speed went for nothing, as State, Stony Man and the security agencies were unable to free up policy clearances until almost midnight.

Stony Man's Hal Brognola had briefed the group in room 224.

"It is, God help us, totally your show," he said. "Win or lose."

Phoenix Force was scattered about the room in varied degrees of concentration. Encizo toyed with his Vzor 7.65, Ohara was doing sit-ups on the floor. Katzenelenbogen clicked the steel claws of his artificial hand in and out.

"No matter what happens," Brognola's voice became more grave, "the outside world must never know this caper took place. The balance in the Middle East is paper-thin precarious, you'd better believe it. I've given this message to Striker every time I've had to brief him—I've done this a lot of times, and I know all about it.

"The message, men, the bottom line—which is

where Mack Bolan lives all the time—is this....
Nobody knows what's going on. You are going to
find out. Nobody else will ever know a thing about it.

"The least of your brief right now is to save the
United States. That's the least of it. If Jeddah is successful in its invasion of American soil, the worst will
soon become apparent.

"I am telling you now that your victory is essen-
tial. It will also be unknown. Otherwise it is not a victory.

"You must struggle like the gods themselves. Your
struggle will become legend—neither true nor false,
but a kind of myth.

"That is your fate in this instance," the middle-
aged White House liaison concluded, slightly lifting
his gray suit jacket by the collar to air his thick neck.
"It is, perhaps, a fate no more or less tragic than the
horror that awaits many thousands of innocent souls
if the Jeddah dragonnade within our borders pro-
ceeds on target."

Hal looked at them hard and sharp. These were
Mack's chosen warriors, the Executioner's own
foreign legion, primed to pounce without mercy to
save that most delicate of flowers: democracy.
Foreign-born but as American as Mack Bolan in
spirit, Phoenix Force was a force that would shoot to
kill. Their defense of democracy would be blazingly
courageous, and they would be unknown for it,
famous only in whisper and rumor, while the flower
continued to blossom, unaware and seemingly unim-
pressed.

The truth of it, Brognola knew only too well, was
that Phoenix Force's job was no different from Mack

Bolan's. Neither of them could ask, simply, what they could do for their country. Mere country did not exist in the rarefied air of national security, where humanity becomes everything and the real global threats are defused in anonymity, in secret, in far lands. Their way to serve was simpler. *They did what had to be done.*

The words echoed in his mind. He thought of Mack Bolan. He thought of the grim reaping of lives in the Executioner's secret world. He thought of the true aim, the true shot (the shot taken and taken right—which is to say *first*), which is allowed Mack Bolan because Mack is the Executioner, the fighter whose enemies are indefensible, the warrior who completes with unavoidable acts the logic of the judge and of the jury.

There is little reward for the new American foreign legion—no promise of citizenship, no place in the history books—because there is none but the most personal reward for Mack Bolan. Phoenix Force is in action for the same reason that Colonel John Phoenix, a.k.a. Mack Bolan, a.k.a. the Executioner is in action: to keep civilization going. With whatever it takes. These people, the Phoenix people, are private beings of violent rebirth.

Hal softened his glare. They were fine men, Phoenix Force. They knew the score—by now they did.... This was their third mission, and by far the stickiest. They had passed their initiation, and now came the goods, the real thing. No more bad nerves. No more false starts.

If Jeddah was getting its goddamned pincers into America's vitals, then the infection must be overcome now. Fast. Unmercifully. Before a fever began and the country's heart was poisoned and the crippled nation state groaned toward grim death.

Red Anvil was the spin-off of Jeddah that so filled with fear the elders of the Popular Front for the Liberation of Palestine that they seriously lost their nerve in the battle of West Beirut. The Palestinians had never been so weak as when their Libyan revolutionary council, Red Anvil, with wild and desperate courage, set out to get the Dessler laser submachine gun from within the United States.

NSA informed Brognola that this endeavor had been identified with Khader Ghazawi, the leader of Libya's Jeddah, ever since he formed the terror group in the mid-seventies. His ambition to secure secret U.S. arms data, research and actual prototypes coincided with the increased development of experimental weaponry in the United States. Jeddah was a pro-Fatah but basically self-serving outfit currently enjoying asylum in Khaddafi's loony bin, Libya. Ghazawi was one of those who knew how to put the screws to the mad Khaddafi.

America's premier achievement, the DLSG, was now in multiple prototype form and, for all Hal Brognola knew at that moment—that extraordinary moment when nothing was known and the clearances had still not come through—the gun could already have been spirited away by Jeddah, be already in a vacuum of chance and terror and rapine soul-theft soon to be filled by a rush of blood from society's avengers. From Phoenix Force.

"These are my orders," repeated Brognola. The overnight neon of El Paso blinked silently, distantly, beyond the curtained window. "We do not move until daylight. Last intelligence reports contained no contact with Red Bluff. Who knows what's going on? No calls going in since 1500 hours yesterday. Total quarantine. Completely unauthorized. One hundred and fifty military and twenty-two civilians locked up tighter than a drum. Your move, gentlemen. Good luck."

Almost at the Red Bluff fence, Katz rattled off last-minute inventory in the rear of the IH Scout. "Manning, grenade launcher? Rafael, the Stoner? David, the AK-47? Keio, your usual? The M-16?" He did a quick visual on his weapon, the Uzi chatterbox he had cut his teeth on. "Grenades, extra magazines, clips for the sidearms...."

Moving with a speed that belied his years and his ass-close-to-the-sidewalk build, Encizo loped forward sixty feet, flung the chain up over the fence with all the grace of a Micronesian net fisherman. The steel settled onto the electrified strands with a pop and hiss. Acrid smoke roiled up, hung heavily in the humid air. Rafael knelt and smugly touched his palm to the grounded fence. "Bring on the dogs," he quoted.

Manning ran forward and wedged a foot to Rafael's thigh, another to his back as Encizo braced himself, then catapulted up to snip and part the barbed wire, all seemingly in one movement. Manning dropped, spun away to avoid Keio as he hurtled down next. He knew cold constriction in his stomach—eternal moment of truth—as he waited for

the chatter of rifle fire, for chopping dismember-
ment. Is this the time I take one?

Manning and Keio sprinted in half crouch for the
low ground that Yak had designated. They hit the
sand again hard, then whirled and panned their
weapons across the nearest buildings. They waited
for gunfire that did not come. Yet.

They heard the thud of boots, and then McCarter
and Katzenelenbogen fell, grunting and gasping,
beside them. They formed a semicircle in the hollow,
poised to fire as Encizo came last over the fence.
Another thump, a reassuring *"mierde"* from Rafael
as he landed, and Phoenix Force was together again.

"Let me check it out, Yak," David cajoled, chafing for action. Chafing for first blood, if truth were
known. "Me and Keio'll come at 'em straight on."

"I don't like the smell of this at all," Yak said,
dismissing McCarter's enthusiasm. He brought up
the Uzi, shrugged his cartridge belt into more com-
fortable position. "We'll stick together on this one,
understood?"

"Check," Manning replied, lifting the CAR-15.
"I'll make lace out of the bastards."

3

There was nothing.

No guards. No dogs. Nothing.

The advance was entirely unimpeded. Then they saw them.

One GI lay facedown, just inside the barrack door, his face badly bruised. Beyond him, in bunk after bunk, laid out like so many corpses in a morgue—

"I'll be damned," McCarter gasped. Rotten, murdering bastards! His mind was racing. Had they killed them all?

Shades of Jonestown. Keio Ohara stood in frozen, incredulous stance, his eyes wide, a rain of goose bumps sweeping his entire body. "Are they dead? I don't see any blood. No signs of a fight...."

They went from bed to bed, looking at each soldier in turn, quailing before the empty unfocused stare in each man's open eyes.

Keio was the first to feel for a pulse. "They're still breathing," he said. "These men are sleeping."

It was Keio, too, who noticed something in the second barrack they hit. "Cigarette odor," he informed Yakov. "Someone was just here."

"We have apparently been observed," Katz said. "Whoever was here has gone, possibly to warn others."

Encizo lovingly advanced the Stoner's selector to automatic. "Didn't like the look of us, huh?" he said with a self-mocking grin. "Take care, *compadres*."

Encizo executed a wide swing to the northwest of the camp—darted from barracks to barracks, then began a sprint and crawl tactic as he hit open country behind the armory buildings. At the end he virtually took cover in shadows in the sand.

Keio and David headed due north, scuttling behind motor-pool buildings. They ducked behind an oil shed, then worked their way toward the front of the depository, relying on parked jeeps and command cars for concealment. A last deep-crouch dash brought them to a cluster of garbage cans stashed inside a four-foot-high concrete block stockade.

"End of the line," McCarter muttered. "Let's see what we have here." He focused the binoculars.

He found his glasses trained on the strangest proceedings developing in front of the depository. "I'll be damned!" He passed the glasses to Ohara. "What do you make of that?"

Keio's scalp prickled, his blood ran cold again. Standing in the glaring sun were approximately twenty-two GIs at parade rest. All stared into space with vacant, unseeing eyes.

To the left, near a smaller building, stood an army officer, flanked by a civilian, both frozen in place as if cast of lead. How long had they been standing like that? Keio marvelled. How long would they go on standing like that?

It was then that he saw that the camp was not empty of the enemy. A small-framed man—wearing fatigues and helmet-liner like the rest—emerged from the bunker with frantic steps and approached the stone-still officer. Keio trained the glasses on him, saw he was definitely of the Arab persuasion. The Arab and the officer exchanged hasty words, then both entered the bunker, the officer moving in disjointed rush.

A moment later three other soldiers broke from the bunker, hot-footed it into the depository itself. Seconds later, they scrambled out with armloads of Colt Commando rifles. They stacked them against the main building and ran back for more. Shortly they hauled ammo boxes into the sunlight, stacked with bandoleers of 5.56mm ammo in twenty-round clips.

"What's happening?" McCarter asked.

"Take a look," Keio said. "They're going to arm the GIs."

"Oh, shit," McCarter said. He peered through the British field glasses. "How many hostiles do you count?"

"Four in all. They're racing to defend their retreat. I guess these are the hardcases who should be guarding the gate. Our presence has disrupted their departure. The rest are long gone. This lot think they can cover their ass with some Uncle Sam GI firepower...."

Keio Ohara, driven by demons, broke from cover and raced two hundred yards in zigzag. One of the Red Anvil hardmen spotted him, brought up his rifle.

Instantly thirty rounds stitched red rosettes all over the jerking body of the Red Anvil hero. Phoenix Force would never miss out on any action.... It was a philosophy that had just saved Keio's skin and afforded him immeasurable pleasure. He grinned his thanks to the four marksmen.

"Manning!" Katz ordered from a distance. "Drop a half dozen grenades on the right side of the building. Diverting action!"

Even as Manning expertly adjusted the sighting-range device on the M-79 grenade launcher from his position near Katz, Rafael Encizo suddenly appeared on the peak of the steeply sloped roof of the depository itself, his Stoner already spitting death.

An Arab released twenty rounds in Encizo's direction before the 5.56mm slugs tore into him from above, into the cranium and down through the upper rib cage, emerging explosively from his back. His body was literally slammed into the tarmac.

The other Red Anvil terrorist broke from the concrete bunker, sought out the unwelcome intruder, opened fire with Colt Commando. But too late, for Encizo was already out of sight.

At that same moment the grenades began dropping, with bone-jarring explosions, to the right of the building. The Arab hit the ground, then frantically crawled inside the depository to rejoin his superior.

Through all the furor, the American troops continued to stand at parade rest, staring straight ahead, oblivious of the slugs smacking around them, of the shrapnel and concrete splinters. One GI's cheek was ripped wide by a speeding chip, but he never moved a muscle.

Keio Ohara seized on the confusion, darted from his position and raced for a heavy steel dumpster vehicle that stood in one corner of the depository loading area, two hundred and fifty feet away.

"Cover me, Yak," McCarter yelled, as he broke for the position Keio had just deserted, the AK-47 bucking as he ran. A stream of white-hot lead emerged from the armory, tore holes in the air three feet above his head.

The American officer, Colonel Ballard, was suddenly pushed from the bunker, an Arab using him as a shield. He screamed into Ballard's ear, and though the words could not be heard at that distance, the resulting action—mime of the most universal and macabre sort—was self-evident.

The GIs suddenly came to life, began firing their automatic rifles in the various directions from which the pestilence of machine-gun fire seemed to be emanating. And though their aim was laughable—eighty percent of their projectiles cruising over the barracks—enough 5.56mm slugs homed in on the scattered Phoenix Force to jeopardize their comfort in this unholy place.

Colonel Ballard continued to bark his commands to fire, and the ground at the robot's feet was soon littered with empty clips. The troops started concentrating on the dumpster where Keio had last been seen. The rapid fire was deafening, the clanging of bullets as they pierced the initial steel barrier sounding like a gargantuan corn popper.

Watching from his vantage point, McCarter knew the dumpster would soon be badly riddled and that freak rounds—bearing Keio's name—would soon work through. And though he loathed himself for his decision, he had no choice. "Sorry, mate," he muttered to himself, "but it's bloody well gotta be done." He trained his AK-47 on the robotized officer, squeezed off four rounds.

Ballard sagged, slid down slowly, his chest a huge bubbling wound. The Red Anvil lieutenant tried desperately to brace Ballard, lest he lose his shield, but the man was too heavy for him.

With a vengeful snarl, McCarter took his time, then deliberately gun-shot the exposed Arab.

The hardman screamed, dropping the slumped colonel, and clutched himself between his legs. His hands came up with yards of ruptured intestines. He stumbled in place a moment longer, then started to sag. McCarter blasted for his head this time. There was a haze of red hatred forming behind David's eyes, but it did not in the least affect his aim. The guy's brains splashed the wall behind him, turning it into an abstract painting of pinkish red and yellowish gray.

The twenty-odd troops reverted to disoriented zombies again. Instead of shooting at the dumpster, at McCarter, they became confused, began shooting into the air, at the building, at the security bunker.

They began shooting at each other.

McCarter and Katzenelenbogen leaped forward, David heading for the bunker, Katz taking the spot just vacated. Even as McCarter ran at breakneck pace, zigzagging in low crouch, the small-framed Red Anvil guy stepped into the doorway, brought up an M-16, zeroed in on him.

The Arab squad leader was a hair too confident, waiting a millisecond too long for the perfect shot. On the roof peak again, Encizo cut loose with his

Stoner, and it was suddenly midnight on the Nile for the terrorist foreigner. His arms flew up, the weapon sailing over his head. The dead man did a jerky buck-and-wing. Now he fell back against the bunker's door jamb, great gaping holes in his chest and abdomen where the outbound slugs had torn away chunks of flesh as big as a fist.

But still the mayhem among the GIs went on. When McCarter dared look up, the carnage nearly turned his stomach. "Dear God..." he groaned. Eight bodies were down, with the rest of the troops spinning in madhouse ballet, like tin toys, their guns firing indiscriminately.

David shrieked the authoritative command. "Cease fire! Cease fire, you stupid fucking apes!"

The men stopped shooting. Score one for military training, more mighty in its effect than any hypnotic. The GIs stared about, seeking the source of command, awaiting further orders.

"Order arms!" David bellowed. Instantly the rifles came down at each soldier's side; they froze in parade-ground stiffness.

But if McCarter thought he had saved the day, he was mistaken. For, at that moment, an unaccounted-for Red Anvil hardman cowering inside the depository opened up on the GIs. It was instant abattoir—four more went down.

A brain-demolishing rage hit David McCarter. Bloody bastards! Outright fucking slaughter! I'll skin you alive, make you eat your own cocks! *"Hit the dirt!"* he bellowed. Instantly the remaining troops dropped to the ground. *"Roll, damn you, roll!"* Simultaneously he sprayed the dark cavern with a screaming stream of 7.62mm slugs, prayed something would connect. There was no return fire. "Keep rolling!" he commanded the pitiful remnants of the GI force, "get out of range!"

From the corner of his eye he saw Keio break for the right side of the main building, with Yak immediately behind him. Above he caught sight of Encizo as he slid down the sloping roof, then floated in graceful paratrooper stance until his legs skillfully absorbed the shock of the twenty-foot drop.

Manning, on the left, the grenade launcher on his hip, was also moving up.

The gathering of the clan, David mused sardonically.

4

McCarter took in the bloody tangle of American bodies in the open space before the door. "Did you catch that action, Yak?" he snarled. "They were bloody well killing each other. Fish in a barrel. Even when I got 'em to stop, the wog tried to finish them off."

The impact of the charnel-house scene was not lost on Katz. But he drew on experience, fought not to dwell on the tragic waste of human life. This slaughter was but a foretaste of the slaughter to come once Jeddah received shipment of the prototype DLSGs. He left the depository area to spark up the radio in the generator building.

McCarter meanwhile brought up the AK-47 and placed a final half dozen rounds into the depository's rafters. Keio and Gary duck-walked forward, stopped just outside the yawning entrance.

"Your last chance, Arab swine," Manning called. "Surrender! Come out with your hands up and you live. Play it smart for once."

But there was only silence.

It was now exactly 1032 hours. The heat of the October day was building up.

"Well?" Encizo said, as Katzenelenbogen returned, striding to where the others now slouched against the wall in recuperation. "What did our State Department say?"

"The usual. We get to play it by ear."

Katz explained that a medical team was en route to unravel the zombie puzzle, as well as attend to the corpses littering the landscape. State had no intelligence of a military convoy leaving Red Bluff. Stony Man, of course, was working independently for them and would forward update as Phoenix moved on. Nothing here was to be touched.

"Sounds like the usual," McCarter sneered with his characteristic cynicism. "I'll look up your asshole if you'll look up mine."

An hour later, loaded into the IH Scout, chomping on K-rations as they tore up large pieces of dreary Texas scenery, Phoenix Force began the tedious foray into the geography of chance as they functioned in tandem with a Bell OH-135 piloted by Jack Grimaldi to hunt down the Red Anvil convoy that had left such a big hole in the Red Bluff Arsenal motor-pool parking lot. They were south of I-20, moving on State 385. Jack Grimaldi was fifty miles north of them.

As they proceeded through the day in a seventy-mile quadrant, venturing into Brownsfield, Plains and Tahoka, they got the same report. A five-truck convoy, sometimes with a jeep lead car, sometimes without, had been seen. They moved fast into New Mexico on 380 when the trail suddenly turned cold in Tatum.

Back to Texas again.

By this time it was 1600 hours; the sun was beginning its seventh-inning stretch. It hovered a half hour above the jagged Guadalupes when Keio monitored the overhead call.

"Do you copy, Phoenix?" came the tinny voice.

"Copy, flyboy. Give your location."

"Highway 180, just west of Seminole," said Grimaldi. The Stony Man veteran sounded true to form, which is to say enthusiastic. "I plot an abandoned factory or something, with a raggedy-ass stretch of landing strip behind it. Maybe a mining company. I'm real high now, to stay invisible, but I'm sure there's some activity here. A dozer working. I can't be certain in this light...it's in shadow already...but I'd swear there are army vehicles down there. All piled up for some reason."

"Roger. Stand by. We're on our way."

Within twenty minutes the Scout reached 180. It hung a sharp right. "Perhaps eight miles on the right," Jack talked them in, "a turnoff—the road's all chopped up. Turn in, go perhaps another mile or so. The dozer's working to the west of the factory, in a deep gully. Can't make it out too good now."

Phoenix Force hit the overgrown abandoned road leading toward the Guadalupe foothills. The Scout bucked and yawed viciously in the rough terrain. The vehicle was in four-wheel drive. Once the smelter stacks and the factory's triple-tiered roof were in sight, Manning killed the engine. Phoenix Force piled out. Moments later weapons and extra gear were unloaded; cartridge belts were snugged into place.

Yak ducked into the Scout a last time, made last-minute contact with Grimaldi, gave wise counsel to back off for the next fifteen minutes to lull the hostiles into false security. "Thanks, eye in the sky," he said to Grimaldi, grateful that Stony Man had come through, as always.

Stealthily they moved out, darting from weed-grown burden heap to burden heap, until they reached a vantage point where they could look down on the curious activity progressing below.

A flatbed carrier, the tractor blue and silver, stood close to an outlying factory building. To the west, snorting, throwing up great plumes of diesel smoke, a Caterpillar D-8 was busily pushing minor mountains of slag to a low bluff and dumping the burden over the edge.

Bolan's men saw why their birdman had had difficulty with positive identification on the army vehicles. The Arab drivers had deliberately steered them off the bluff, into a gully where the five trucks now lay in topsy-turvy scramble like toys in a sandbox. The Cat driver was putting finishing touches on his graveyard chores; another two dozen passes and the trucks would be buried in gravel forever.

"It's what's known as covering your trucks," muttered Encizo.

Katzenelenbogen suppressed a grin, concentrated on scanning the terrain below with his binoculars. "There are only two of them standing guard," he said. "Only two. They are dressed in working clothes. Once they're done, they'll load up the tractor, then hop in the cab and melt into the night. Another ten minutes and we'd have lost them for good.

"The DLSGs are long gone, I suspect," he

grunted. "They must have had a fleet of small aircraft coming in and out of here to carry out that much stuff today. They're probably loading a truck in Piedras Negras at this very moment.

"Therefore, gentlemen," Yak continued, unmistakable need in his tone, "it becomes imperative that we take one of those fanatics alive. I'm sure that, between us, we can coax him into talking."

He turned hard, decisive. "Keio, work through the buildings on the right. Get into those slag piles behind them, then work your way down. Hand-to-hand if you have to. Bring me a live one."

And to Encizo: "Cross-country for you. Try to work in from behind also. David and Gary—move through the buildings with Keio, but split off, try to take that driver. He's the most vulnerable, he won't be able to hear over the noise."

Katz indicated a shallow streambed just below them. "I'll try to close in from there."

Moments later the five men were melting into the fast deepening gloom.

The abandoned lead mining plant made for unusual terrain. Flitting swiftly between and around the small mountains of slag and overburden, Ohara, McCarter and Manning reached the factory proper within minutes. Waiting for their eyes to become accustomed to the early dark, they cautiously drifted through the complex, Gary and David scuttling down a long aisle of ore sorters toward the bulldozer, Keio continuing between two buildings, heading for the high country again.

For long minutes Gary and David crouched just inside a smashed-out window, looking down to where the bulldozer, its driver oblivious to their presence, diligently huffed and puffed. They caught a glimpse of Keio to the far right as he went up a steep hill, hands clutching the sere grass like a monkey, covering the terrain in fluid dartings. They saw him circle behind the lone Arab sentry, actually put down his M-16, take out the thin, black, silk garroting cord he was so skillful with. Now he crawled, foot by foot, toward his unknowing quarry.

Keio was perhaps fifty feet from the Red Anvil sentry when Manning noticed a blurred movement behind his buddy, and saw an Arab "sleeper" melt out of a niche between two boulders, M-16 poised, smilingly drawing bead on Ohara.

"Goddamn!" he breathed, torn for the briefest moment between his orders from Yak and his loyalty to his comrade-in-arms.

But if Gary hesitated, David did not. In one continuous move, gracefully swift, he slapped off the safety of his AK-47 and took sight on the hardman who was savoring his cheap shot. "Keio!" he roared at the top of his lungs. The AK-47 bucked and roared in his hands, years of practice helping to keep the weapon from climbing. He emptied half his thirty-round magazine as Keio instinctively ducked from the warning. His trajectory was true, a solid skein of death, the 7.62mm slugs catching the hardman high, opening up bloody faucets in his body from brain to crotch.

Even as the sharp chatter ricocheted off the mountain walls, echoing its litany of counterterror, the

Arab that Keio had been stalking whirled and cut loose with his M-16. The ground erupted—miniature volcanoes—just six feet in front of Keio, lending wings to his desperate leap for lower ground. He hit rolling—going ass over teakettle—kept rolling, the M-16 spitting death inches behind him.

5

By the time Manning had opened up with his CAR-15, thinking to chop the hardman down before he finally zeroed in on the dazed Ohara, the Japanese warrior's escape became problematical due to an inopportunely placed boulder.

For the briefest second the would-be Arab patriot was torn between two elemental desires—to blast this infidel off the face of the earth, or to save his own mangy neck. Self-preservation won out as he sent a desperate burst in Manning's direction, then flung himself to the left, instantly dropping out of sight in the same crevasse he had previously used for his hiding place. There was a loud clatter of pebbles and small rocks as he made like crazy for the low country.

Gary dropped down the incline like a goat, fell beside Keio where he lay in a heap, totally still.

"Keio, buddy," he groaned, the fear suddenly large within him that the lanky Japanese had finally caught one. "Are you okay, KO?" he sang in alarm. He saw a glaze of blood along the right side of Ohara's face.

Keio's eyes blinked open then, and he smiled groggily at his distraught friend. "Now I know," he said groggily, "what it's like between a rock and a hard place...."

Both men slapped fresh clips into their rifles as they tumbled unsteadily down the rocky incline. In the encroaching gloom they caught sight of Encizo and McCarter in jarring, zigzag, in-sight, out-of-sight pursuit of the Arab runaway.

By the time they had worked their way to the right of their buddies, the Arab had gone to high ground again. Short, precise bursts from his M-16 effectively pinned down Rafael and David.

"Up we go, Gary," Keio said softly, his face grim with determination that he would be the one to track their quarry down.

"I'll pin him down from here and from above," murmured Manning. "Give you a chance to close in from his blind side. Can you handle him alone?"

"You think I spent the money instead of going to karate school?" smiled Keio, wiping his cut and blood-smeared cheek with an impatient hand.

A moment later he had melted into the shadows. Manning began eyeballing his movements through the piñon bushes and stunted, gnarled spruce, between the jagged outcroppings of rock, but quickly lost sight of the elusive Oriental. He ran obtrusively to the lee of a huge boulder. "*Mano-a-mano*, huh?" he grunted to himself. "Take him alive if he can!"

In minutes, Manning infiltrated a rocky stronghold three hundred feet above where he was crouched. It was a tough climb as the seconds of remaining light ticked away.

Evidently the Red Anvil hardman was prepared for a long siege. A handgun of indistinguishable origin at his right, a double bandoleer jammed with clips of ammo directly before him, he was absorbed in taking leisurely potshots at Encizo and McCarter, who were letting him believe he had them pinned down.

The irony was not lost on Manning, and a dozen times he drew long, careful bead on the Arab, thought how lovely it would be to eliminate him at any given moment, to see his head explode, should Manning but choose to touch the trigger of his specially doctored CAR-15.

Down below him he could barely make out the bulldozer driver still busily at work, still oblivious as he worked to complete his heavy duty.

Keio should be close enough to make his move by now. Within killing range. Where he could bring those kill-proficient hands of his into deadly play.

Movement to the right, and Gary came alert. The Arab saw it too, sent a short burst of M-16 tumblers in that direction. Protected by the distraction, Encizo revealed himself to Manning, sent guarded high sign that he had now spotted Manning's stronghold. The word would go to David.

Showdown was at hand.

Keio Ohara could hear the Red Anvil flunky stirring in his eagle's nest directly above him. Concealed just beneath a rocky shelf that protruded from the side of the hill, he was protected from Phoenix fire. Even so, he still had good view of Rafael and David. And although Gary could not see him, Keio could fix him in his sights whenever necessary.

For long moments he studied the terrain between him and the lip of the Arab's stakeout; he memorized every foothold in the five-foot expanse of stone, pinpointed where each successive hand grip would fall.

He adjusted his M-16, secured it to his back.

He waved down to Encizo and pantomimed a hands-around-the-neck gesture, then pointed up to Manning. Encizo nodded, gave Gary a sweeping indication as to where Keio was holed up. Simultaneously Keio leaned back beneath the shelf to stand clear of the harassing fire to come.

Manning opened up, a lazy pop-pop-pop. The slugs were skillfully patterned, revealing just enough of his position to whet the arrogant hardman's appetite. The Arab spat back with short, teasing bursts.

Three strides—every movement sure, precise, his breathing suspended—and Keio was at the top of the incline, hanging to the lip of the enemy's lookout with powerful fingers. Gary Manning drove in three more rounds, closer now, forcing the Arab to concentrate. And then, abruptly, he let his fire die.

The brown man wondered for the first time whether he had been duped. But even as he stole a glance to his left—Keio attacked from the right.

His hand slammed down with the force of an Automag slug. It caught the enemy alongside the neck, all but severing his clavicle.

Sheet-fire detonated within the terrorist's brain, screaming pain blotting out all else. Flight, self-preservation, retaliatory action—none of these options registered. Only the mind-blitzing pain remained! The rifle was seemingly propelled from his hands as it flew over his head and caromed off the lair's precipice, to clatter down the mountain.

And before he could *think* of going for the automatic that lay in easy reach—the bombshell hand came in again with freight-train impact. He knew his right cheekbone was fractured. Again a thousand arc-lights gapped in his brain.

"I surrender. No more...please! Stop the hit...."

Keio's movements were fluid, reflexive, and the lightning-swift sequence of kicks, kneeings, hard-finger thrustings deep into the opponent's gut were seemingly preprogrammed. Keio struck a half-dozen more times before he cinched back the violence.

Now the Arab groveled on the ground, vomiting.

Keio stood over him, gripping the man's arm behind his back, reassured that his skills in the martial arts had been of use to Mack Bolan's American foreign legion. He heard the thump of boots on stone as Phoenix Force hurried to join him.

It was here that he made his mistake. If compassion is ever a mistake.

"Mercy, *effendi*," the Arab gasped, prone beneath Keio's merciless nelson grip. "For the love of Allah, show mercy...."

Ohara loosened his grip a mere micro-torque. From within that brief relief, the crazed man lurched. Was it ritualistic self-destruction, or terror-stricken escape from pain? Maniacally he whipped himself loose and upright. With fleet steps, and with Keio off-balance, the quarry was suddenly gone.

And over the edge. It was only a drop of a hundred feet or so from the treacherous, darkening aerie—the body bouncing, rolling, careening into open air the last forty feet of its freefall—but it was sufficient unto its ends. There was an ugly snap, a gelatinous wet plop as the Arab hit the wide ledge below and came to full rest.

Encizo reached him first, looked up accusingly at Keio as the Japanese scrambled down to join him. There was no reason for close examination, but Encizo lifted the battered head briefly from the stony ground, studied it, dropped it in a definitive move.

Tarique es salame—the man's journey of peace was now at hand.

They left him there, wearily began working their way down what remained of the incline. Men of action to the last, they did not put words to their frustration.

Except Keio Ohara. "They beat us again," he intoned, "they beat us again."

The dozer driver still slammed levers, lurched back and forth, putting last touches on his gigantic burial project. The army trucks now lay beneath at least four feet of hard-packed dirt.

Breaking from the shadows of the smelter staging area, Phoenix Force fanned out, seizing relative cover behind the flatbed trailer and beyond.

The scowling driver, released from his chore, suddenly arose from behind the controls and started to pull levers fiercely from a standing position. Expertly he locked the tracks, spun the Cat completely around. He put the hydrostatic shift on full, blasting forward at twelve miles per hour. There was death in his heart.

Manning and McCarter scattered left and right. Tractor and flatbed would go in one shearing, twisting tangle of steel. Now the Arab driver brought up his M-16. It penciled bright orange fire in the dusk.

David McCarter whirled and loosened a half-dozen rounds himself. The fleshseekers hammered the steel engine and whined off into the sky. The death-driven driver prepared to jump off the Caterpillar, then clumsily slipped as he did so.

The Arab pitched forward in a slow-motion dive. He landed lurchingly on a moving track. He was instantly sucked forward, abandoning his weapon, and as he fought to recover, his left hand was pinched in the rolling track plates. He screamed as his fingers were devoured by the merciless steel. Now his whole body was dragged forward in viselike grip and flung over the front decline of the cleats. He was pounded into the ground beneath the tracks, reduced to bloody, flattened meat within seconds.

Then the tractor hit the truck, its twelve-foot blade pushing the one-tonner over on its side. The Cat stubbornly began shoving the vehicle across the yard, grinding its driver into ever greater degrees of liquidity as it did so. When trailer and tractor hit the factory wall, bricks crumbled, steel screeched. Still the huge dozer chewed up the ground, dug in, until finally the engine was killed, and went still.

"What a way to go!" commented McCarter.

New action sickeningly erupted all about them. From the distance a surprise M-16 opened up. Pieces of brick and plaster rained down on Phoenix Force as a Red Anvil last-ditcher shot high and wide.

"Another hero coming at us," McCarter hooted. "Where'n hell they all coming from?"

Six more rounds homed in at the Englishman, closer this time. More splintered brick coated his fatigues. Even so, thinking to at last fulfill Katz's fondest wish—to bring him a real live assassin—

McCarter deliberately held his ground, goading the slap-happy fanatic still further.

Lead blasted the walls above him, then to the right of him. Where had the bastard learned to shoot, he thought. With a Girl Scout troop?

McCarter dropped, came up again, purposely presented irresistible target. He dared the desert commando to empty his weapon.

"Damned fool," Encizo roared at McCarter, moving off to the left, hurrying to outflank the gunman.

Keio was close on Encizo's tail. Manning was hotfooting it toward the right. From a somewhat distant overlook in the hills, Yak came floundering forward on the right, to join forces with Manning.

All but McCarter headed toward a cluster of boulders located five hundred feet up on a low rise, where the latest damned Arab had chosen to make his stand. The four men dashed and dropped, dashed and dropped. Each man held his fire.

Alive, take the bastard alive!

Preoccupied with his hit-the-McCarter-doll game, the mutton eater did not notice the tightening ring until it was altogether too late. By then Encizo was a scant thirty-five feet away, crawling fast, Stoner ready to blast the terrorist to hell should he ever commence to pose real threat.

The Arab's M-16 clicked out of ammo. Staring about in panic, seeing the hard-eyed quartet almost upon him, remembering his orders not to be taken alive, he made his decision.

Terror time!

Grisly, self-destructive rite was instantly performed. The zealot had whipped forth a .45 automatic from within his baggy clothes. He charged it, jammed it into his mouth. One tug of the trigger, one muffled report, one last kick as the back of his brain went spinning into orbit—

He too was gone to that great goat roast in the sky.

In the dispatcher's office at main headquarters at Reese Air Force Base, in Lubbock, Texas, a scant seventy-five miles away, First Lieutenants Bob Driscoll and Tom Mathers were frantically rifling through the day's sorties. Object: To find a missing piece of government equipment. In particular, a Lockheed C 141A Starlifter, one of their biggest transports. Recently returned from Marietta, Georgia, where it and all its sisters in the air force fleet had been lengthened to carry more cargo, it had been back on line only two months.

Now it was gone.

"There was a manifest here earlier today," Driscoll said. "I saw it myself. Now it's gone. Call Lieutenant Childress in here."

Childress, commissioned a mere four months, was a likely scapegoat and scared shitless. A twenty-million-dollar transport missing? And he was responsible?

"They had legitimate orders, Lieutenant," he defended, "signed by General Jellico himself. Major Beames, Captain Thompson were up, an eight-man flight crew altogether. They had a ten hundred hours takeoff, with orders for a twenty-two-man detail to load and accompany top-secret cargo. I double-checked the orders, even called headquarters. They verified a priority clearance. How can the manifest

be missing? I filed a copy right here. . . ." His fingers
rifled through the manila folder, came up empty of
the desired documents. "I don't understand. . . ."

"Where were they cleared for?"

"Hanscom, in Bedford, Massachusetts."

"Well, get cracking. Put them on alert. Hold that
plane when it touches down. No mistakes this time.
Something strange is going on."

But the Lockheed C 141A was not headed toward
Massachusetts. It was flying at twenty-two thousand
feet over Huntsville, Alabama. The flight was slightly off schedule due to a refueling delay at Ricken-
backer Air Force Base in Columbus, Mississippi.
Final destination: Langley Air Force Base, Hamp-
ton, Virginia.

In the cockpit of the monstrous transport a
swarthy-skinned officer leaned over the seats occupied by the pilot and copilot, chatted softly in
Arabic with the flight officers. "Ahmed," Lieutenant Ramos complimented, "the landing and take-off
were excellent. Amazing how much you learned in
just three months. Do you have qualms about landing at Langley? Will there be any problems with traffic control?"

"I think not," replied the dark-complexioned first
officer. "I will not overlook radio procedures."

"See that you don't," Ramos replied. "It's too
late now for mistakes. They will be looking for us at
Hanscom Air Force Base. Meanwhile we will be unloaded and gone before anyone at Langley is the
wiser." He chuckled thickly. "Ghazawi's plan has
worked to perfection thus far. Allah is good."

"Allah is good," repeated the pilot.

To the rear, in the great yawning superstructure of the Lockheed, sprawled among the one hundred and eighty crates of superweaponry, were eight corpses, dressed in underwear, piled in a heap to one side of the loading floor. All had been executed at close range, the hole behind each man's ear neat and tidy, the work of a Beretta 84. They lay in scrambled disarray, congealed blood, flecks of gray pulp in a puddle beneath them, the bodies not even accorded the simple dignity of a GI blanket.

The remaining eighteen members of the Red Anvil strike force slept or talked softly, congratulating themselves again and again over the success of the day's work. They paid the dead bodies no heed whatsoever.

6

Agonized howls erupted when the entire Red Bluff contingent was quarantined to base until further notice. No word of the bizarre developments could be allowed to leak to the outside world. The arsenal and all surrounding grounds were declared off-limits; army teams combed the terrain nonstop—truly a Keystone Kop caper.

When outside questions arose concerning Colonel Ballard, Ben Harper and the other fourteen GIs killed on Tuesday, the interested party was told that they had been abruptly transferred. Further questions were stonewalled. Next-of-kin were informed that the dead men were merely "confined to quarters indefinitely" (and more confining quarters than a pine box you just don't get).

The investigators ran into obdurate dead ends.

Those troops who woke up under guard in the camp infirmary, who in pain wondered about bullet wounds, broken fingers, missing parts of their anatomy, gashes and other abrasions incurred during the arsenal firefight, were given no answers at all.

Thus the army psychiatrists found themselves working overtime.

Strong sedatives were prescribed for those survivors who awoke screaming in the dark, racked by nightmares in which they watched nonstop reruns of themselves shooting away the faces of closest buddies—unreality perversely bridging that temporary erasure of memory.

And as for the six Red Anvil hardmen they had scraped off the depository tarmac—

They were buried before the maggots had time to set up a reception line....

Norfolk, Virginia. Hectic loading activity was winding up. At Pier Forty-Three the USS *Beaumont* was standing by for early departure. On the subchaser's forward deck Lieutenant Commander Maxwell Endicott conversed with an officer wearing army dress greens. Both men looked down at the dock, watched as a work detail loaded aboard the unmarked rectangular crates that had arrived by truck convoy shortly after noon that same day.

"This comes as a bit of a surprise to me, Lieutenant Ramos," Endicott said, openly miffed by the abrupt change in orders. "I was told this would be a mere shakedown cruise. My orders indicate a stop at Naples, with a precipitate return. There was nothing said about a standoff at Tripoli."

He indicated the work crews below. "It took some doing to requisition extra rations, to allocate quarters for the twenty troops in your party, for you and Lieutenant Sandoval. I wish those nitwits at base would give a guy more warning."

"I realize it's an inconvenience, Commander," Ramos said, his tone mild and persuasive. "My men will pitch in, they will do their share of the work."

"Classified stuff, you say?" Endicott winked at

Ramos. "Can you give me an inkling of what we're carrying? Electronics? Uranium mining gear?"

"Sorry, Commander," Ramos smiled. "As you said, classified. All I am privileged to reveal is that you will not be putting your crew into jeopardy because of its presence."

"Well, all I can say is it's one helluva note. We've got a sixty-six-man complement, and your twenty-two brings it to eighty-eight. We'll be taxing the facilities more than a little." He unfolded the freshly cut orders, studied them again. Then he shrugged and turned to leave the command deck. "Orders are orders, I guess."

7

McCarter, monitoring stakeouts in Tampa, Pensacola, Jacksonville, Miami, Key West and dozens of backwater outlets to the Gulf, had uncovered nothing.

In Mexico, scuttling between Monterrey and Mexico City, keeping tabs on action at Matamoros, Tampico, Veracruz, on the west coast too—at Mazatlan and Manzanillo—Encizo relayed matching negative report. *El zilcho grande.*

Manning, in charge of contacts in Corpus Christi, Galveston, Port Arthur, New Orleans and Mobile came up empty.

With Stony Man's extensive resources, with help from the CIA as well as a half-dozen other federal agencies, Katzenelenbogen and Ohara also scored zero. They had pored over shipping manifests, departure schedules, run down bloodlines on every cargo ship moving into the Atlantic in days. They had scoured the New York docks, drunk in scuzzy seamen's bars in Baltimore, Philadelphia and Portsmouth, scrutinized the Charleston and Savannah portside scene.

Stakeouts on virtual bivouac at Tripoli's Airport International reported no suspicious activity there. The same for Wheelus Air Force Base, formerly U.S. property, now a terrorist staging area. Nothing that in any way resembled weapons crates was moving in or out at either site.

"They might have gone to ground," Hal Brognola shrugged as he conferred with Yak mid-afternoon Friday. "But I'm betting they're on the high seas at this moment. Those bastards want to move those guns real fast."

"Where's our weak link?"

"You tell me. It has to be staring us right in the face."

"So, what are the orders?"

"We'll let you do some ocean reconnaissance of your own," Hal replied. "Departure schedules indicate only fourteen vessels falling into the time frame. You have authority for a board-and-search— especially if you run across something out there that's not on our list. Hope you guys have got your sea legs."

Thus, at dawn on Saturday—Encizo the last to straggle in—Phoenix Force crammed aboard a Bell HH-1K. Within seconds of boarding, the craft slowly lifted off its pad at Fort Eustis, Newport News, Virginia.

The two officers assigned to the search mission wondered what the hell was going on with these guys dressed in dark-olive camouflage jump suits, armed to the teeth. Did they really know how to handle that array of automatic weapons?

The pilot shrugged. It was no skin off his nose. Taxi drivers, that's all they were. They knew home base, they had a fix on naval support ships for refuel operations; they could safely patrol for days without returning stateside. A long list of the latest coordinates on running ships was strapped to the pilot's knee. Other than that they were under orders to Colonel Katzenelenbogen.

The Bell HH-1K with Lycoming T53-L13 engine was capable of a top speed of one hundred sixty, and had a range of over three hundred miles. Designed primarily for sea-air rescue missions, the whirlybird was more than a match for any cargo ship wallowing along the four thousand miles of Atlantic sea-lanes at eight to ten knots per hour. During the first three hours at sea, it overtook three freighters.

One of these, an ore-boat of Chilean registry, loaded with phosphorous, was not on the master list, and was promptly boarded. The helicopter came to land, precariously, on an aft loading hatch.

The black mustachioed captain was not pleased with the visitors from the sky, but under U.S. Coast Guard proviso 14 US Code 141B, which provided for interaction of governmental agencies on the high seas, there was not much he could do to protest the boarding and search.

But Captain Archuelo's bad humor was quickly mollified by Rafael Encizo, who shortly had him smiling, then laughing as he joked with him, first about the search, then about Chilean political conditions.

By the time Manning, McCarter and Ohara regrouped from their fast lookaround, Katz was satisfied as to the legitimacy of the freighter's manifest. "All clear," McCarter reported. "Hell, even their can opener's dull. Not a weapon anywhere."

As the helicopter lifted off, Archuelo stood on the deck, waving goodbye. Rafael returned a friendly salute from his seat behind the copilot.

"Knock it off, will ya?" McCarter mocked. "Christ, you get two beans together and right away it's old home week. They start swapping fart recipes."

By noon the Bell had intercepted three more cargo ships. On a freighter carrying machinery to Poland, a Russian ship taking precious American wheat home, a U.S. merchant ship transporting chemicals, they had found no unauthorized cargo.

So went the rest of the day, with the army helicopter zigzagging the sea-lanes, working its way east by gradual degree. Twice they had paused to refuel aboard naval support ships steaming for Gibraltar, then gone on. Always as they crisscrossed the sullen ocean, there was update from Stony Man relayed through military wavebands.

"Needle in a haystack," Gary Manning said gloomily at 1600 hours. "I think we're just chasing our damned tails."

"Oh ye of little faith," Katz intoned with wintry smile. "If Stony Man says they're out here, then it must be so."

He addressed the copter pilot. "Let's find lodging for the night. My calculations indicate the *Nimitz* is nearby. Right?"

"Yes, sir. En route to the Med. She's at thirty-six degrees, fifty-six minutes north and sixty-two degrees and twenty-six minutes west. That's roughly thirty knots northeast of our present reading. We'll be there in twenty minutes.''

There was diversion at that moment. A low-slung naval vessel, its grayish, bobbing hulk almost directly west—silhouetted against the cutout redness of the sun—hove into view. "I'm not familiar with that configuration," Yak said. "What kind of ship is it? Certainly looks like it's seen better days.''

"It's an old subchaser," Captain Innes replied. "The U.S.S. *Beaumont*, recently recommissioned.'' He indicated his knee chart. "She's on our list. The class has been mothballed since the early sixties. I expect it's a shakedown cruise to see how her engines function.''

At 1630 the Bell HH-1K was being paddled to a landing on the *Nimitz*'s main approach strip. After their precarious drop-ins on various cargo ships all day, the vast spaciousness of the stadium-sized deck and the crisp efficiency of the carrier's landing batallions seemed like the big time to the chopper's passengers.

Phoenix Force emerged from the Bell to find a junior officer waiting to greet them.

"Now this is more like it," David grinned as he gazed at the ten-story superstructure that loomed above them. "Welcome to the Atlantic Hilton.''

Khader Ghazawi, flanked by Janda Yamani and Emida Sarafid, were on the *Beaumont*'s control deck when the helicopter passed over. Noting the hover-bird's brief deviation in course before it had finally sped southeast, he felt a twinge of uncertainty.

Everything had been going smoothly for Jeddah, and it would be absurd to have its plans disrupted because of some nosy army reconnaissance.

"A search party?" Yamani queried.

"Most likely," Ghazawi said absently, speaking in Arabic. "I imagine the Atlantic and Mediterranean are covered like a blanket." He laughed softly.

"My compliments once more, my brother captain," Yamani said, his gaze encircling the ship's nerve center, taking in the Arab helmsman at the wheel, while Lieutenant Commander Endicott slumped in a nearby chair, his face blank, his eyes staring, unseeing, at the opposite wall. "Your plan is sheer genius. I see no way that Red Anvil can be stopped now. There is no way our *jihad* will fail."

"And yet you argued with me, Janda," Ghazawi needled. "You would have had us fly the American plane directly to Libya. Then the might of the American Air Force would have descended on us like avenging eagles in a matter of hours."

"Forgive me. When I think of our holy cause I lose good sense."

"Please remember that confusion is our greatest ally," preached the Jeddah leader. "Once you have your enemy off balance, you keep him that way. An idea planted in the Western mind becomes akin to writ. The Americans have developed a way of looking at things that clouds their brains to the possibility of alternative actions. This is their greatest frailty.

"A huge airplane like the one we, ah, borrowed in Texas is not so easily hidden, and when it failed to turn up in Massachusetts as scheduled, the alarm was surely not long in being sounded. And that could have proved fatal had we continued to fly it across the Atlantic.

"This ship was the wisest possible course. We could be on the sea for weeks, and they would never suspect what had happened." Again the mild laughter. "Especially with our American sailors so well under control."

The forty-year-old man who stood gloating over his stratagem was not as dark-skinned as Yamani and Sarafid; also he was overweight, with an air of indolence about him. This was a deceptive facade. There was no overt threat, no menace attached to such an unkempt, waddling ragbag as Ghazawi. Or so his adversaries thought, right up to the moment their throats were slit, or their heads blown away by the Walther PPK—the automatic he favored, and carried always in a specially fitted holster inside his baggy jacket.

His slovenly front was partly responsible for Ghazawi's success and longevity with such terrorist factions as the Arab Rejection Front and Black September. But even that fanaticism had been too mild, too laggard for Ghazawi.

Enter Jeddah.

Enter a bloodbath, a bubbling molten caldron of messianic bloodlust that would not be sated until the civilian streets ran red with innocent blood.

Khader Ghazawi had come aboard the U.S.S. *Beaumont* shortly after the subchaser had entered international waters. He had been delivered by a speedy cruiser owned by a wealthy Irishman highly placed in U.S. government circles—one of a number of rich dumb fuckers whose money bought them the

thrill of Jeddah's illicit and anti-Semitic cause. By the
time Ghazawi was aboard, the evening meal had
done its ugly work; and officers and enlisted men
were piled up like cordwood in their bunks all over
the ship, and Yamani and his specially trained cadre
were in total charge.

Other well-placed contacts in key positions had
created the original smokescreen of misplaced vital
manifests, stolen data, providential access. The
American bullheadedness referred to by Ghazawi,
both in its purposeful way and as it had expressed
itself in the total secrecy clampdown that stubbornly
prevailed at Red Bluff, worked in the Arabs' favor.
Then, once the recommissioned chaser had left the
yards at Norfolk and crucial departure functions
were done, Yamani's shock force had swiftly insinu-
ated itself into the fabric of the vessel's routine.
Feigning helpful curiosity in the galleys, they had
managed to disseminate ample quantities of the
thorazine and GB/Sarin mixtures into the evening
mess.

Within two hours: Instant replay of the eerie hap-
penings at Red Bluff Arsenal forty-eight hours
earlier. Sailors dropped like flies, watch and duty
calls went unanswered. Solicitous terrorists had
gathered up those who collapsed short of their
bunks, tucking them into chemical cold storage until
such time as their robot skills would be needed. On
the bridge, the helmsman, the lookouts and quartermaster of the watch found themselves suddenly too
weary, too befuddled to carry on. They smiled in
grateful stupidity as the mahogany-complexioned
newcomers volunteered to take over their posts.

The transition was silken-smooth. The Red Anvil trainees knew naval equipment inside and out. Other than the interruption when Ghazawi had come aboard, the *Beaumont*'s husky diesels continued to push a steady fifteen knots and never skipped a beat.

Now Ghazawi and Yamani smiled in smug unison as they saw the shuffling line of sailors begin to form outside the enlisted men's mess. The gobbies, wearing heavy pea coats, braced against the chill October wind, moved forward sluggish foot-by-foot as Jeddah hardmen badgered them unmercifully. Eventually the line began to disappear into the mess compartment.

One of the last of the sailors, a tall barrel-chested youth of twenty or so, stumbled against the rail. A sadistic Jeddah officer ran at him, punched him viciously in the mouth, shoved him back into line.

And though the blows flung his head back hard and caused a thin trickle of blood to run down his jaw, the lad was oblivious to the pain, to the humiliation.

Any other time he might have made mincemeat of his pint-sized tormentor.

But this day he stared straight ahead, his eyes vacant.

8

Phoenix Force was under way once more at 0730
hours. They had covered a quadrant of roughly six
hundred miles yesterday; today they would do better.

All had spent a restless night, each member of the
team drifting in and out of sleep, jerked to wakeful-
ness by the slow pitch of the carrier, left to hover on
the razor's edge of sleep, dogged by specter of failure.

First on the agenda was the unlisted Arab freighter. A six-knot wind was snapping the carrier's flags
as they climbed into the Bell HH-1K, made careful
ritual of inventorying and repositioning their gear.

Silence prevailed for an hour as the copter worked
its way toward the Arab merchant ship, the cabin
warming slowly in the thirty-eight-degree weather.
The grim-faced warriors could as well have been
sculpted in stone, each holding cramped, stolid pose,
staring into space, lost in dark private thoughts.

By 0930 hours the freighter, *Sullim III*, was
sighted; the helicopter headed down. Radio contact
was established. After eight minutes of parley, the
commander was convinced to allow them to come
aboard. As the Bell's skids touched down, slid, then
came to firm rest on a rear deck littered with lashed-
down crates, the captain came forward with surly fire
in his eyes.

Yak emerged, the Uzi submachine gun poised meaningfully. All starch went out of the Arab in an instant.

Keio and David were in the hold for almost a half hour. When they came out, disappointment registered on their faces. They found Rafael and Gary already waiting, matching their looks of frustration.

Two more tramp freighters—refined oil for Norway, beef for Germany—were overtaken and boarded before it was time to head for a naval fuel tender. As before, they came away with nothing. By then it was noon. There was brief break for lunch, courtesy of the U.S. Navy.

Back and forth, through that endless afternoon the copter shuttled across shipping lanes, dropping down on cargo ship after cargo ship.

The second patch-up of the day to Stony Man granted no reassurances. "Keep pounding away," Brognola's voice came in scratchy volume.

Katz sighed heavily, broke radio contact. He stared out to sea, clicking the steel fingers of his prosthetic device in abstracted rhythm.

Once again the sun rolled its way westward, hovering an hour above the horizon.

It was as Yak conferred with Captain Innes, checked coordinates, and made radio contact with the naval vessel that would berth them for the night, that Encizo stared morosely down at the Atlantic and saw a U.S. naval ship perhaps two knots east. He identified it as a minesweeper, heading stateside. Fleeting vision of Teresa crossed his mind, and he knew aching desire to be on that ship, heading away from this no-win standoff.

He allowed his mind to glaze over, easing into a

cerebral twilight zone. His thoughts were in drift as he looked down at the minesweeper cutting its wide, sluggish V through the gray green ocean.

In half trance he visualized the search copter dropping down onto the vessel's foredeck, all of them hurtling out, swiftly deploying themselves for a search. It was a dazed extension of the day's wearying routine, a thing akin to those times when the day's fierce activities carry into the sleeping state, and one drives, skis, plays tennis all night long.

An electric tingling sparked at the base of his neck. It sizzled through his scalp, was relayed down his back and arms.

Oh, Jesus holy Christ! he exclaimed inwardly. Why hadn't they seen it from the start?

"That's where they are!" he blurted. "They're aboard one of the navy boats!"

His four comrades jerked up from private reveries.

"Where would Jeddah expect us not to look?" raved Rafael. "I tell you, the U.S. Navy is carrying contraband for Jeddah!"

The Cuban's mind spun crazily, spat out another wild card.

"That's why we couldn't find that stuff before. We were looking for private planes, for private trucking companies. Why bother, when you can use U.S. Air Force boxcars?"

His voice rose an octave. "The action at that abandoned mine? All bullshit! Right then they were winging across the U.S. in an air force transport."

"How? How?" Manning interjected urgently. "How would they engineer a thing like that?"

"The same way they engineered the infiltration at

Red Bluff. Inside stuff. Key men in strategic positions, cutting phony orders, authorizing special flights. They air-freighted the laser guns to an east-coast base, then transferred them to a naval vessel. You tell me where the biggest naval base is, that's where they loaded them!"

"What are you on, Rafael?" McCarter scoffed. "You mainlining chili sauce?"

But then David read the concentration on Yak's face and fell silent. Keio Ohara had also gone into hunched trance; David could almost hear the mental computer clicking as his brain collated the plus-minus elements of Encizo's stunning hypothesis.

Now Keio looked up, his black eyes blazing. "But to what purpose the transfer of the weapons to a naval vessel? Why not fly straight through?"

"Because," Katzenelenbogen offered excitedly, "that missing air force transport would light up Strategic Air Command war boards all over the world. SAC would scramble, they'd ride them down in neutral territory or shoot them out of the air."

"C'mon now, Yak," David insisted in his jeering Cockney accent, "don't tell me you're buying this bag of smoke."

For perhaps a minute and a half Katzenelenbogen stared out to sea, his brows furled, his steel claws tapping in restless tattoo on the cockpit frame. Then: "Try for a transmission to our Virginia contact," he commanded the copilot-navigator.

Excitement continued to run high as the Bell HH-1K spun on its rotors and headed for the night's roost aboard the U.S.S. *Dauntless*, a submarine rescue ship located forty miles due east. Yak's conversation

with Brognola in the remaining seconds of flight
sealed their fate, and that of the U.S. Navy, and that
of the criminal Red Anvil, for the next incredible
day. The wheels were in motion. One more call and
the action would be confirmed.

Katzenelenbogen sought out the commanding officer
of the *Dauntless* the minute they crawled from the
cramped helicopter, firmly commandeering the vessel's radio shack.

It was 1736 hours before he reappeared, his face
grim.

All Phoenix Force members looked up expectantly
from their places in a distant corner of the host ship's
mess hall, expressions wary. Their food—mostly un-
touched—still sat before them. McCarter smoked a
cigarette; the rest sucked at cups of strong black
coffee.

"Congratulations, Raf," Katz announced as he
poured coffee. "You called it perfectly." His eyes
reflected respect. "I, personally, am indebted."

There was a moment of silence, all eyes fixed on
Encizo, who sat with a stiff smile on his face, for
once at a loss for words.

"Tomorrow, gentlemen," Yak announced, "we
take on the U.S. Navy. All clearances have just been
approved by State."

The briefing that followed was given in clipped,
unemotional fashion. Apparently the right people,
backed by strong intervention from State and advice
from Stony Man, had come down—totally hard—on
the commanding officers at Langley and Reese Air
Force bases. Total revelation or else! Cages had rat-

tled down the line of command until the weak links were flushed. The conspiracy of silence would result in the most effective possible formal charges. If firing squads were still in style, they'd have been damn busy right away.

The most despicable cover-up had occurred at Langley, right at the seat of the CIA, where the abandoned Lockheed Starlifter had languished for forty-eight hours before official inquiry after the missing flight crew had been instituted.

"How many men?" Keio interrupted.

"Eight," Katz replied. "We assume they're dead. Probably feeding the sharks by now."

"Bloody Jeddah bastards," McCarter spat. "They'll pay."

"There was an attempt to hush the matter up at both bases," Katz continued. "Covering their asses. 'An internal matter' was how they excused their blunderings. But then, how *does* one own up to the responsibility for a missing transport? The fools thought the whole thing would blow over...."

9

The commander of the *Dauntless* gave Katz and company the expected mouth-full-of-fishhooks grin when they asked permission to search the hold. But by then he had received instructions from central operations at Norfolk; there was no argument.

He assigned a junior officer to accompany them belowdecks.

And because they could not afford to take a chance, once they got below, each Phoenix member carried his assault rifle at the ready position.

"This thing," said Gary Manning, "is like asking your mother who your real father was." The crewmen eyed the international armed gang with deep suspicion.

"Tell me about it," Keio muttered grimly.

The time-consuming search uncovered nothing. Coming up from the holds, Phoenix Force again ran the gauntlet of tense stares as they moved in their combat fatigues, weapons drawn, expressions brazenly blank, toward the helicopter.

There were seven possible naval vessels to be boarded, but Norfolk had narrowed priority to three that fell into the category that Jeddah would most likely commandeer. They were the U.S.S. *Bolster*, a minesweeper, the U.S.S. *Glacier*, a salvage ship, and the U.S.S. *Beaumont*. They were all in the same quadrant; they could be reached comfortably in a day's time.

Last-minute coordinates were radioed to the copter, and Phoenix Force was airborne again at 0914 hours. There was an hour's ride between them and the *Glacier*, the nearest ship on their list.

Again, they landed on the salvage ship's afterdeck and emerged with weapons poised, ready for World War Three, there were the scowls of suspicion from a startled crew.

Again the search was a monumental waste of time, and Bolan's warriors came away with renewed anger and frustration.

The minesweeper was next. It was nearly noon as the Bell made its approach. Katz surveyed the vessel through binoculars.

"You have clearance," the ship's radioman said crisply to the Bell's copilot. "Come aboard. You're just in time for noon chow."

Phoenix was predictably wary as the HH-1K copter slowly settled on a clear area on the foredeck. Their eyes darted, looking for the slightest tipoff that they were dropping into a trap.

The five men jumped from the hoverbird and swiftly deployed themselves in preset security pattern. The waiting gobbies unsuccessfully tried to cover their curiosity, their resentment.

The XO saluted Katz from the bridge while a second officer hurried forward to meet the unsettling "inspection team."

The sweep took a mere twenty minutes. The MSO was only one hundred seventy-two feet long; there was not that much extra space for hiding contraband available.

The helicopter was away again. Now for a two hundred mile jump, due west. Destination: U.S.S. *Beaumont*.

It was 1420 hours when the lumbering subchaser, top speed eighteen knots, was finally sighted.

The skies had turned leaden en route, and a patchy fog was building.

The *Beaumont*'s decks were deserted. Except for the dark shapes visible on the bridge, the SC gave the impression of being abandoned.

Yak's mouth drew to a tight line. "Hover at three thousand," he told Captain Innes, "but keep out of firing range. Her guns should be deactivated, but we can't count on it."

Then to the copilot: "See if you can raise somebody on board."

"Calling U.S.S. *Beaumont*," the lieutenant rasped into his face mike. "This is U.S. Army four-two-four-two-one-zero, directly at starboard. Under provisions of naval directive G-three-twenty-sixty dash J, we request permission to come aboard. U.S.S. *Beaumont*, do you read me?"

There was a moment of silence, and then the dash receiver crackled to life. "Permission is denied," the voice said. "Any attempts to land will be met with force. We will shoot you out of the sky."

"Repeat," the radioman replied, "we are acting under provisions of priority orders, naval directive G-three-twenty-sixty dash J, which authorizes boarding and inspection of your vessel. Failure to respect this order will result in. . . ."

"Failure to keep away from this ship," a new voice retorted, "will result in your being shot down, do you understand?" The voice was strident, unmistakably accented. "We are not being boarded."

At that moment recognition flared in Katz's eyes; they filmed with fierce hatred. Unhooking the mike from the lieutenant's neck, he pressed it close to his mouth. "Is that you, Ghazawi?" he growled. "Khader Ghazawi? I thought you'd be back in Libya, you creep, cowering under Khaddafi's *burnous*."

There was momentary silence. "Who do we have here?" Ghazawi said, his tone uncertain. "Katzenelenbogen, is that you?"

"It is, Ghazawi."

"Well, well," the voice crackled. "I thought we had got you in Beirut. My agents told me you were dead."

"Your agents are wrong," Yak taunted.

"We got your bastard son in the Sinai," sneered the voice from below. "Too bad we missed you."

Yak reddened, the vein on his forehead pumping. "You don't have a chance, Ghazawi. I advise you to heave to, surrender peaceably. I work for the Americans now. I will have part of the Atlantic Fleet in range within a matter of hours. And they will blow you out of the water."

"Will they? Aren't you forgetting something, you camel turd? I have sixty-eight American sailors and officers here. They all die if you even *try* to board this ship."

Yak's face went dark as death. Yet he held his peace, cheated Ghazawi of satisfaction. "You are a creep to hide behind innocent men," he said evenly.

"It proves to me that you would collapse and sing like a cowardly woman at the first touch of my knife. I know about that time in Cairo, Ghazawi. You have little to boast about."

"Silence, *Jehudi* swine!" the Arab exploded. "You try my patience!"

"We will stop you at Gibraltar," Katz hammered on. "Those weapons will never be delivered."

"Won't they? Do not bet on it, you licker of American ass! The guns will reach my brothers in the cause. We have our ways." He snickered again. "The Americans are fools when it comes to human life. They will never risk the mass murder of the personnel aboard this ship. The world will never forget America's spineless performance in Iran. I should fear your powerful navy? Your jets? Not while I hold these men."

They heard him address someone in the background—muffled Arabic commands. And then his voice scratched again through the speaker: "You think I am not a man of my word, Katzenelenbogen? You have binoculars with you in that toy plane? Watch. Here is firm proof of my intentions."

Encizo and Ohara trained the glasses they held on the *Beaumont*'s starboard deck, saw a bulkhead door open, noted six uniformed sailors march out in robotlike lockstep. "Yak, stop him!" yelled Encizo.

But there was no stopping the brutal act. Ghazawi's voice screeched from the radio: "Two, this time." The sound of two pistol shots, tinny and faint, carried next. Encizo's fingers tightened on the binoculars as he watched. He saw the gout of blood and gray matter explode from the opposite side of each man's brain. He saw the way some of the gore splashed a nearby sailor, was amazed that the man never flinched as his face ran with blood and pulp, his eyes focused straight ahead, neither the gruesome act nor the close-range report of the weapon cutting through his stupor.

From three thousand feet Phoenix Force and their crew saw the bodies slump slowly. They saw an Arab leap forward and lift each body over the rail.

They fell as if in slow motion, bodies twisting, down through the twelve feet from the deck to the ocean and into the brine with a splash, floating briefly, the water turning dark with blood around each sailor's head. And then they began to sink.

"Another?" Ghazawi's rasp taunted the very airwaves. "Shall I order another to be shot? If you do not withdraw immediately...."

Yak numbly signalled Captain Innes to wheel, to put distance between the copter and the subchaser.

"You'll pay for that, Ghazawi," he said into the mike. "You'll pay for it with your own blood. You'll wish you'd never been born. I swear this and you had better hear it clear."

10

Brognola, in the Stony Man war room, listened to Yak's report with impassive calm.

"Regroup at the *Dauntless*," he ordered. "I'll have navy operations on it now. We'll box them in at safe distance, and stand off temporarily. I expect we can get the *Nimitz* to heave to, be ready to provide fighter support or whatever—if we need it."

Brognola's mission was to maintain Phoenix Force's cover, to keep them secret from the moment they went into action of any sort, to protect their covert strengths from the eyes of the populations of the world the minute they made their move—thus protecting them from the compromises that were inevitable when the media were in on it, when the top brass were forced into screwing around with something that, to put it simply, called for real men in real war.

"Request permission for a night boarding," Yak said, his voice thick with frustrated attack. "There's cold-water gear aboard the *Dauntless*."

"Be back on that soonest," barked Hal. "Roger and out."

For the second time that day the Bell HH-1K settled down on the deck of the *Dauntless*. Though it was dusk, and the wind was raw and biting, crewmen still worked abovedecks to see their arrival. And though these crewmen could not possibly know of the afternoon's grim action, they could most certainly sense a dramatic change.

The five men who unloaded this time were haggard and preoccupied. The dull anger in their eyes, the hard set to their mouths was warning enough. Something drastic had happened.

Gathering in one of the three officers' cabins assigned to them after chow, the five men discussed battle plans.

A daylight boarding attempt was out of the question. The drugged sailors would be wiped out, their Jeddah keepers squashing them as callously as they might roaches beneath their feet.

It was already too late for an attack tonight. Phoenix Force must continue to dog the *Beaumont* all day tomorrow, keeping out of sight, lulling the Arabs into believing their blackmail had worked.

Keio Ohara suggested a night parachute drop at close range. A copter, flying so high its engines could not be heard, would drop them ahead of the *Beaumont*. They would regroup, wait for the subchaser to close on them. Swift swimming, a hasty boarding action, and then—

"By then, cold-water suits or not, we'd all be dead," countered Encizo. "That water's forty degrees already. None of us would stand a chance."

"A submarine, then," McCarter offered. "If we surfaced close enough, we'd be all over the bastards before they knew what hit them."

"None of our dispatches indicate a sub within a

thousand miles,'' pointed out Yak quietly. ''They'd have to start one from Gibraltar.''

At that moment a sharp rapping at the door summoned Katzenelenbogen to the *Dauntless* radio room.

His face was somber when he returned. ''As we expected, gentlemen, it's our baby. Washington and Stony Man have decided. We go aboard tomorrow night. We minimize our losses insofar as humanly possible. One consolation, however.''

''Yes?'' Manning said.

''Their prayers go with us.''

At 2320 the following night the specially rigged Bell HH-1K prepared to lift off the *Dauntless* foredeck.

The rotors slapped up a deafening roar as the ship's crew watched apprehensively. And though they had no inkling of what was about to take place, all sensed grave danger was involved. Just watching the plastic-sealed parade of weaponry go aboard the hoverbird in the night had been indication enough.

Cold slanting drizzle glistened on the black exposure suits that the hardbitten gunfighters wore, gave them even more menacing presence, made them look like black phantoms, avenging angels.... The assault rifles held tightly to each man's chest shone dull as wet slate as Phoenix Force boarded their helicopter.

The rotors revved, churned the ear-numbing noise to higher pitch. The vortex plastered the deck crew's clothes to their bodies, mix-mastered their hair. Now the copter climbed slowly. It slid away from the ship's superstructure with long cables trailing from its skids.

The moment the copter reached twenty feet, the deck men scuttled forward to steady the already charged IBS attached to the heavy lines. Six sailors strained to keep the black inflated rubber float from gashing itself on a forward bulkhead. Then all the long lines went rigid, and the precariously swinging raft cleared the last obstruction.

The copter shot up swiftly. The clumsy boat faded with it, and disappeared altogether into the pitch-black night.

The ship's crewmen bolted for cover from the rain, each man breathing fervent thanks that he was not invited to that particular party.

In the dark cabin the men of Phoenix Force sat in silence, occasionally wriggling within the constricting wet suits, brooding on the bloody firefight facing them. A greenish flicker came from the control panel, now giving their blackened faces the likeness of demons rather than angels.

Katzenelenbogen made last-minute check on the AN/PRC 10 mobile radio that was strapped, along with his Uzi, to his bulky chest. The unit had a twelve-mile range, which was more than adequate for maintaining radio contact with the copilot—should things get too hairy, should instant recovery prove necessary.

"Keep watching those bearings," he called over the harsh roar of the engines to the navigator. "Five miles is absolute minimum. The wind's out of the west, it should help muffle our noise—but let's not take any chances."

The lieutenant readjusted their course by perhaps half a degree. "Wilco, Colonel." Their responsibilities weighed heavily on the crew; they might wish that someone with the secret reputation of a Jack Grimaldi could do this job for them, but Grimaldi was a Secret Operations Group flyer and needed elsewhere, and their crew was not inclined to shirk the obligation to act as part of the John Phoenix group, who could and should fly proud for their country.

Making a wide sweep of the U.S.S. *Beaumont*, the copter hit top speed, heading for a designated point precisely seven miles ahead of the subchaser.

"Approaching jump zone," the copilot-navigator warned loudly. "Two minutes." The copter began its descent.

The combined racket of the engines and the slapping rotors was awesome as McCarter slid aside the back bay doors on the copter. The wind tore at his comrades' hands and faces. They shuddered despite the heavy wet suits, the insulating underwear beneath.

"Geronimo time, chaps," McCarter shouted.

When the Bell reached an altitude of twenty feet, it hovered in as stable a position as the ten-knot wind would allow. David yanked the release cable and let the IBS drop to the roiling ocean below him. A blast of wind threatened to overturn the two-hundred-eighty-nine-pound, twelve-foot-long hunk of rubber as it fell. But at the last moment it flattened out and landed on the waves with a dull splash, its motor still firmly in place.

Encizo lumbered forward, embracing his Stoner M-63. He checked to see that his ammo was secure, then tightened his life preserver one last notch.

He saw Yak's thumbs up, and scrambled from the

cabin, braced his feet on the skid. With a grunt, he dropped, caught the skid with his hands, hung on. A last glance at the angry sea below, and he released his grip, dropping like a sack of sand.

He hit the water hard and went completely under. The impact was like someone had landed a haymaker to his gut. And cold! How could water get that cold and not turn to solid ice!

As he surfaced, he kicked with the flippers that he wore over his canvas shoes, fighting to close the fifteen-foot gap between him and the current-driven rubber boat.

His wet suit swiftly took in water, chilled him further, made him clamp his teeth with pain. He kicked more fiercely to narrow the distance. He groaned with relief as his body became somewhat numbed, even warm from the water now contained next to his body, preventing further heat loss for the moment. Minutes later he reached the tossing raft, expert as he was at aquatic activities. Then he wrapped his hand in the life line and lurched up into the IBS.

There was no time to catch his breath. In precise, practiced moves, he scrambled around the edges of the boat, disengaging the drop line.

Now, with the lash of the copter's rotors tearing at him and chilling him anew, he stood and braced his legs and readied himself to catch the line already being lowered from above.

Then it was in his grasp; he swiftly snapped the clevis into the towing bridle. Immediately the boat began to turn slowly, straining against the anchorage of the hoverbird. The line went taut, holding at a thirty-five degree angle.

A minute later Rafael felt vibration on the line, and prepared to assist Manning, the second man down; there was no need for the rest to take a dunking if they didn't have to. In the murky half-light he saw Gary working down the line in swift hand-under-hand.

Encizo steadied his colleague, gave him a vicious yank at the last moment to keep him from going over backward into the icy water.

Both waited for McCarter, then flung the new arrival inside the raft with combined strength.

David unstrapped an extra supply of grenades for Encizo, and moved to take his place at the upraised outboard motor. Straightaway he yanked the starter cord to pop the seven-point-five horsepower engine to life. It barked, sputtered, then revved to throaty roar, propeller free of the water. Now he adjusted it to a rich idle, and finally to a gentle purr that could hardly be heard over the wind.

Keio Ohara was the next man down. His right foot slipped on the slick rubber, and he howled as he got a soaker. He cursed at himself.

All four men watched with admiration and mutual pride as Yak came down—Uzi and ammo and radio all strapped on. He straddled the rope with his right armpit, controlled his slide with his good left hand. The way he zipped down, no one would ever suspect he was an amputee.

Shortly Katzenelenbogen was on board, issuing terse commands.

"Cut us loose, Encizo. Ohara, arrange the grappling lines."

Yak clicked on the radio. "All members down

safely," he reported to the crew above him. "Retrieve the landing line. Stand at prescribed distance until further word."

As the line popped loose from the towing bridle and slid upward into the copter's bay, the IBS yawed wildly, spinning on a huge wave. "Bring us about, McCarter!" Yak bellowed.

"Aye, aye, Captain," McCarter whooped, expertly turning the boat to meet the waves at proper angle. "Wahoo! Better'n a roller coaster any day!"

Above them the helicopter pivoted on its rotors to climb due east, then stand watch three miles ahead of the drifting rubber boat.

McCarter smoothly maneuvered the IBS across the six-foot swell. "Throw-up bags are in the pocket directly in front of you," he quipped. "Call your stewardess for any further assistance."

"Keep the motor at minimum thrust," Katz ordered. "Enough to keep us right side up. Ohara, drop that sea anchor, see if you can slow us down a little more."

As the copter noise faded, and only the wail of the wind and the splatter of the rain on their suits could be heard, an almost overpowering sense of isolation came over the group. Should their readings prove inaccurate, they could drift all night and never be overtaken by the subchaser.

"Oh, sweet Mary," Manning groaned each time they crested a swell, then began sliding down the other side, "mother didn't raise this boy to be a sailor."

Again there was silence, the enormity and ruthlessness of the ocean confirming the puny insignificance of their strength against nature's lifeforces.

For forty minutes the IBS drifted. Yak was braced at the stern, searching with his binoculars for some distant pinprick of light every time they crested a wave. And finally, when it came, his: "There she is!" took his fellow fighters by surprise and made them jump. "On our right, about a mile off!"

Each man came instantly alert. Five pairs of eyes sifted the darkness for first sight.

Still on the binoculars, Yak relayed directions to McCarter in a steady, monotonous flow: "Keep her right as much as you can. Right, right. Now left a bit. We want to be right in her path. Left a little more."

"If I could just see the damned scow..." griped David.

Again the AN/PRC 10 was flipped on. "Target has been sighted," Yak advised. "Back off, maintain a five-mile distance until further contact."

Hands tightened on the safety lines, on the plastic-encased assault rifles. All members of Phoenix Force could now see the ship's running lights. Yak ordered the sea anchor to be raised.

Time, gentlemen.

McCarter cut the motor, started it, cut it, adjusting their course time and time again. The muffled glow from the bridge grew brighter. Now the low-slung subchaser was altogether visible, bearing down on them at a considerable rate of speed. Two thousand feet. One thousand feet.

"Motor," Yak called.

"They'll hear us for sure," David warned.

"Chance we'll have to take."

The IBS closed in on the subchaser from the starboard side. Black suits, black boat...the assault team was just another part of the black ocean. They could see the prow plowing a huge swale in the water: dark figures on the bridge became plainly visible: the muted bulkhead lights revealed nobody on deck. Nobody to hear the gasps of bruised life and the clang of iron hooks that were about to sound in the wet night.

Five hundred feet. Two hundred feet.

"Baby that motor," Yak barked. "Encizo, Ohara, stand by with the grappling lines. McCarter, Manning, brace us for impact."

A feeling akin to death-chill filled them. A puny rubber life raft was all set to bang against the side of a multi-ton ship traveling at fifteen knots, at the mercy of the wake and then of the steel-plated ship itself. Could they pull it off?

The boat was rocked furiously. David kicked the motor hard, achieving a degree of stability. Now the craft was ladled inward, tossed toward the *Beaumont*. It tipped into a long lazy swoop. Devastating collision was seconds away.

Moments before they hit, Rafael and Keio whipped the grappling irons upward. They hung in midair at twenty feet, dropped onto the deck with a muffled thump.

Instantly the two men cinched one line in the towing bridle, the other to the inside safety line. The whole complex of moves was like an unbroken process, a dance of life at its most extreme, a display of exactly what Phoenix Force was all about.

The raft bounced into the side of the ship with stomach-churning impact. Each man clung to the safety line. McCarter on the motor was swung around hard, so he threw up his feet to buoy himself in the base of the boat, which was now sliding along the crusted hull.

The raft veered inward, then out, half tipped by the pull of the holding lines as it was whipped into tow. Everybody scrambled toward the inner wall of the boat to keep it from capsizing.

Perhaps ninety seconds passed before the IBS stabilized itself and the threat of capsizing was behind them. Now the IBS was slapping along insanely, though at an even keel, not unlike a toboggan behind a speeding pickup. Yak ordered the hand magnets into play. David and Gary grasped the handles of the magnets tightly, placed them gingerly, grunted against the sudden strain as the circular plates sucked themselves to wet steel. The men stiffened their grip, grimacing with exertion as they won even more stability for the careening boat.

"Ladder, Encizo," Yak hissed.

Up went the rope ladder from Rafael's mighty hurl, its specially padded hooks hovering above the rail a foot or so, coming down, then being instantly snugged back hard. Encizo snubbed the ends of the ladder to brass rings on the safety line in a swift half-hitch, and adjusted them to proper slack.

The grappling lines towing the IBS, drawn taut at a forty-five degree angle, had rendered safe boarding nearly impossible. But the rope ladder hung at the perpendicular.

The only threat now was that first looksee over the rail.

First man up might fall away with a bloody stump for a head.

Encizo glanced to Katzenelenbogen, his eyes shining luminously in his sooted face. Chilling rain spattered his wet suit and hood in dull tattoo. The Stoner's plastic waterproofing rustled in the sweeping wind. "Now?" he said.

Katz nodded. "Now!"

McCarter strained to hold the raft as steady as possible in the wild conditions. "Here's to hell," he issued the traditional battle send-off.

"And to all her ugly little children," added a grim-jawed Gary Manning, stolid Canadian white man sending his best to his swarthy Cuban confrère.

Rafael Encizo slowly fought his way up the twelve-foot length of rope ladder.

11

The ladder swayed, went slack and taut in turn, making footing treacherous. The climber carried a Stoner M-63, a satchel containing a dozen grenades, a knife, a Vzor 7.65, plus a Beretta Brigadier for good luck. No wonder the ladder quivered.

Down in the IBS, all watched his shaky ascent, saw him pause just beneath the lip of the rail. Rafael's head darted up, shot down again. It craned up a second time, swiveled cautiously.

Then he threw a leg over the rail, slid over, fell out of sight.

Instantly Katz was up. Though all longed to climb with him, to assist him should he falter, none dared face the testy rebuke they would receive for their pains. They marveled at the deft skill with which he handled his artificial hand, twisting the steel claw in the swaying ropes, finally reaching the rail to pause momentarily. They watched as his arm went over, deposited the radio. Encizo, huddling close to a bulkhead, covered him. Then this mission's bossman went rolling over the rail.

Keio Ohara followed, then McCarter, with Manning put to the real test as the last one up who had to keep the ladder from whipping. His climb was the most dangerous of all. But he was one of the most rugged of all men.

Each warrior's battle station was branded on his brain; all day long they had studied navy blueprints detailing subchaser layout. Now each of them crouched in shadow, hastily tearing away stiff plastic to free up weapons and grenades.

There was terse review. Most importantly: Find the enlisted men and officers, fence them off from outright slaughter. That was top priority.

Encizo headed forward soundlessly. His assignment was to get onto the bridge unseen, to count noses and evaluate firepower.

Ohara and McCarter were sent belowdecks to check out the berthing compartments.

Manning was to reconnoiter the engine room; to bring the subchaser to a lumbering halt would be an ace card.

Katzenelenbogen would scout up the officers' section, most likely site for those of the off-duty Jeddah hardmen who might currently be sacked out.

"Unless all hell breaks loose," Katz ordered the three men, "regroup here with Encizo. If you do draw fire, get back to the crew berthing areas. We'll make our stand there."

Encizo was moving with catlike speed down the deck, only his canvas shoes slightly squishing as he ran. A noise from the bridge froze him. He ducked back under the captain's gig where it hung in davits just behind the stack.

Above him loomed a fifty-foot-high communications mast, showing only running lights at its peak. Beyond that, eighteen feet above the decks, was the bridge.

When the sound was not repeated, Rafael edged

out and padded on toward the bow. He had come at
the bridge from the front, where Ghazawi's troops
would least expect him. When he reached the gun
mounts—mothballed twenty- and forty-millimeter
antiaircraft guns starkly silhouetted over his head—
he backtracked.

With a soft grunt he collided with some crates
lashed to the deck. He rolled onto the rear gun mount
and began working his way toward the bridge, only
twelve feet above him now.

Reaching a forward ladder, he drew the Vzor 7.65
from his belt, checking the safety. He began climbing
upward, one slow step at a time. Upon reaching 0-2,
he dropped to his knees, commenced crawling around
the bridge bulkhead.

Hugging himself into the shadows, he crabbed past
the bridge doors, then ducked into a murky alcove between the mast and the bridge superstructure itself.

Rafael paused briefly, waiting for any sign that his
movements had been spotted. When he was sure he
was safe, he crept forward again with painstaking
care. His face in shadow, his body at least a foot away
from the rain-streaked glass, he stole a look inside.

The men's backs were to him. He moved in closer.
There were no U.S. naval personnel inside—the three
men on the bridge were as brown as a mule's ass.
Even better, all were inattentive. One Arab dozed
openly in a chair, his feet up on the helmsman's rail.
Another leaned against the wall, eyelids drooping.
Only the helmsman, staring straight ahead into eter-
nal darkness, seemed alert.

The two drowsy characters were armed. Each
sported an M-16, one rifle leaning against the wall,

the other balanced across the sitting man's lap.

Rafael silently questioned Yak's orders. A pull at the door, three neatly placed shots with the Vzor automatic, and three animals would be screaming their way to hell.

But no, reconnaissance only. Slowly he lowered his head and began retracing his steps.

Edging past the double doors, he felt the distinct twinge of a golden opportunity missed.

Now he was easing down, careful not to set up giveaway vibrations through the steel ladder.

There was no real need for Manning to descend all the way into the bowels of the *Beaumont*. The noise that poured out as he opened the hatch was so loud he could have rolled a beer barrel into the engine room and no one would have heard it.

Like some north-country *ninja*, the heavyset man on nimble feet went down one level on the ladder and ducked back into a murky offset. Here he had a good view of the activity below.

The heat from the hammering diesels swarmed up, caused his wet suit to turn clammy with sweat. He knelt and leaned farther out over the deck opening. Three American sailors stood before the gauges, staring at them with unblinking concentration. Behind them two Arabs sprawled in chairs, one alert, the other glaze-eyed in near sleep.

Manning's eyes darted, quickly spotting the M-16s stacked in a nearby corner. Any shooting here, he judged, would result in deadly ricochet. And the swabbies would be cut up like so much horse meat.

He started back up the ladder.

At that moment, in the narrow corridor just outside the officers' rooms, Katzenelenbogen was suffering a distinct case of the jitters.

Something was out of synch here. A chilling tremor braced him.

He had first listened outside each stateroom door, straining to hear sleep sounds—a snore, a muttering, even conversation between Jeddah guards—but he had heard nothing. Next, with Uzi poised, he had gone so far as to crack a few doors, peering inside.

In every case he had discerned only dim outline of two supine, drugged U.S. officers, identifiable because of their mussed dress blues. Down the line he went, opening door after door. In each room, two officers, nothing more.

And where, he wondered, large amazement growing, were the Jeddah and Red Anvil headmen, who by rights should have commandeered the officers' quarters? There ought to be a dozen of them here at least.

In the last doorway, which led to the officers' wardroom, his search was rewarded. Instantly Katz stiffened, his finger fretting the Uzi's trigger. Even in the muted glow, he could tell. The four men at the mess tables, their rifles close at hand—Arabs, and no mistake.

But where were the rest? He moved on silently, scouted two more officers' compartments, found only American personnel.

The cold breath of the unknown grew stronger.

Keio and David were equally mystified. As they prowled the forward and aft berthing compartments, they found only doped enlisted men, no Arabs.

Down corridor after corridor, unnerved by the sight of the three-tiered bunk installations filled with their complement of seemingly dead sailors, the two men proceeded with the stealth of angels in hell.

"None of them wogs is minding the store," snarled David. "What's comin' off here, Rice Man?"

"Beats me," Keio replied, his face tense, eyes ablaze, ready for any Jeddah who might pop from the gloom. "Spook City. Let's get back, make our report."

Crouched in a ragged semicircle about Katzenelenbogen at midships, each man tersely provided his head count of hardmen.

"Three on the bridge," said Rafael softly. "Half asleep. I saw two M-16s."

"Gary."

"Two in the starboard aft, one in port. Three Yanks in each. Three M-16s."

"Keio. Davey."

"Zip," McCarter muttered. "We counted fifty-six sailors, all of 'em drugged out. No wogs anywhere in the berthing areas."

"I counted ten officers," Yak said, "and four Jeddahs."

"Ten Arabs in all," Gary spoke up with disturbing finality, head bowed in the rain. "Where'n shit are they hiding? The real heavies, I mean."

"That's a good question," Yak said. "And if I know Ghazawi, he'll answer it for us sooner than we'd like." Yak arose to full height and made decisive adjustment to his ammo belt. "McCarter and

Ohara, hang back," he ordered. "Those sleeping sailors are your responsibility. You both have the anger and the fire in you to never give an inch. We need that from you now."

And to the rest: "We'll see about freeing up those officers. Three of us can handle four terrorist pigs."

"You know it, Yak," Manning said simply. "Lead off."

The three avengers started down the deck in a half crouch, shortly disappeared through a door that led into the enlisted men's head. The compartment was lit only by dim red standing lights at each end.

"There's a passageway here that feeds into officer country," Katz instructed. "They're dozing at a table in the mess hall. We'll take them before they can grab their weapons. This way. Keep your distance."

Yak's strategy was doomed.

Just as the trio entered the connecting passageway, an Arab flitted into view, fastening his trousers as he came out of the officers' head.

He froze, his eyes exploding at the sight of the weirdly garbed men, black shiny fish carrying firearms, grenades, knives.

"Wakkif! Min inti?" the terrorman blurted, as Yak leveled his Uzi on him.

Rafael yanked his knife from its sheath and hurtled toward him for silent death, but the man had darted away and flung himself into the wardroom doorway. *"Hasib, hasib!"* he screeched. *"Amrikani! Amrikani!"*

Yak broke for the door that the Arab had slammed behind him and gave it a quick yank. At the same time he fell away to escape any fire from within. When none came, he dropped to his knees and fell forward onto his belly. Snaking the submachine gun around the steel framing, Yak ducked his head into the opening, then instantly pulled it back. When he drew no fire, he inched forward, took a more deliberate look into the wardroom.

In the eerie red-tinged gloom he sensed movement at the wardroom's far end. He heard the dull clang of another door there. "Gone out through the galley," he seethed. "Manning, come with me. Encizo, make with a backtrack and herd them in before they scatter."

All hopes for a silent takeover were summarily dismissed as Yak broke through the galley, slammed open the steel door, simultaneously darted back into the protection of the adjoining bulkhead.

In the nick of time—for a Jeddah killer on the other side drilled a half-dozen rounds through the doorway.

Committed now to a very noisy—and bloody—firefight, Yak dug out a grenade with instinctive precision, and pulled the pin and released the handle. Holding the old-style (but so effective!) pineapple for brief seconds, he lofted it upward into the passageway to explode in midair.

The timing was perfect. Sharp metallic concussion followed careening shrapnel that ricocheted wildly inside the steel coffin. Deadly ricochet. A shower of scrap iron, of blood and gristle began raining down before Yak risked emerging from his back-away.

He poked his Uzi into the opening and sprayed an arc of 9mm slugs into the darkness. There was no return fire. He burst through the door, flung himself against a bulkhead, threw another grenade onto the upper deck.

A second explosion tore the night apart.

Yakov and Gary Manning clambered up the ladder and rolled onto the deck and were up and running in one fluid movement.

Manning slipped on a slick of blood and gray white pudding matter, looked down in anger to see the pulverized remains of a once human head.

Sounds of firing carried from up front—the flat, almost deceiving chatter of M-16s, the clang and whine of ricocheting slugs.

Katz and Manning came onto the deck through a hatch behind the stack. "Watch it!" Encizo roared from above their heads. The two men hit the deck and rolled to the right, just as an M-16 on the bridge tore the hell out of the whaleboat to their left.

Encizo was crouched behind a shielded 40mm gun mount perhaps thirty feet behind them. The unleashed Cuban sent a five-round line toward the bridge. The Stoner set up a racket like starting time at the boiler factory. The bridge glass fragmented into glittering popcorn. Interlaced with the clamor was a gurgling outcry and the clatter of a falling assault rifle. Clutching his face, one of Ghazawi's finest did a slow dive off the bridge, hit the starboard bulwark, caromed off into the icy sea.

A loud whoop sounded behind them, then McCarter's AK-47 began stuttering its blood song. More glass in the bridge superstructure shattered.

Inside, the Arabs were crawling on the floor, begging for Allah's protection from double and triple banks of flesh-seeking slugs. "Here's hot sauce for your next sheep roast, you bloody bastards!" David roared happily up at them as the ear-splitting clang of lead bouncing off inch-thick armor announced the arrival of streams of 7.62mm tumblers at the *Beaumont*'s nerve center.

Desperation mixed with idiocy caused one Jeddah hardman to pop up in the window, to send a batch of bullets at the gun mount where Encizo was holed up. The slugs spattered against heavy steel with a sound like bolts in a cement mixer.

The volley provided distraction. Suddenly there was flitting movement to Gary Manning's left. "Someone's heading forward!" Manning called. "I'm going after him. Cover me."

Yak came around the stack on the right side, let his Uzi thunder, angling shots into the bridge's ceiling. "Encizo!" he called. "Is Ohara forward?"

"Affirmative!" Rafael howled against the wind.

"The engine-room gang is on the loose. Guard those American sailors!"

Manning's natural night vision now at maximum efficiency, the Canadian crept forward in stealthy crouch, seeking the elusive Jeddah trooper. Abruptly he froze, his heart jamming in his throat. As he saw the enemy poised behind a packing crate, even now raising his M-16 to blow Keio away where the Japanese stood outside the door leading to the EM's quarters, he made a decision of a millisecond's duration.

If Manning should miss, or if his shot should be deflected by the steel and kill his comrade—and so the Mark I trench knife was in his hand. Without hesitation, like an express train he flung himself across the deck at the Keio-occupied Arab, hitting him just as his finger began to curl on the trigger. The knife should have penetrated his throat and half decapitated him with one plunge. But the Arab had spun at the last moment, and his canvas gunbelt deflected the blade.

The Arab grunted a curse, tried to bring his weapon up to fend off Manning's next thrust. But Gary was faster in every way. The dagger handle, hard as brass knuckles, slammed into the side of the hardman's face, shearing away a six-inch flap of skin. The man fell sideways with a scream. His rifle clanged on the deck.

"Gary?" Ohara yelled into the blackness.

"Freeze, Keio," Manning called. "I've got him."

The Arab was not through yet. In last-ditch despair he went for Gary's eyes as he tried to drive his knee into Gary's groin. Manning ducked, swiveled, caught the blow on the side of his hip. Again he hammered the swarthy, pain-distorted face, heard a splattering sound as a Levantine nose was all but torn away.

The maddened Arab had no counter for Gary's next move. Manning ducked halfway beneath the staggering body, twined his left arm around the man's knees, locked his right hand in a steellike grip on the enemy's right bicep. With a grunted lift, Gary raised the body almost level with his head, meanwhile dropping one knee on the deck and the other leg out like a balance bar.

He brought the body down on his knee like a heavy branch to be broken. The Arab's spine was centered perfectly, came down with immense impact on the trestle of flesh and bone. There was a distinct snap, an astonished, sucking gasp.

Gary rose, stood over the dropped body, watched with cold satisfaction as the Jeddah hardman flopped and writhed in agony. A moment later, blood pouring from his mouth, he jerked a last time. Another late check-in at Motel Allah.

Keio whispered softly from the shadows. "Looks like *something* I taught you stuck...."

Up on the bridge another foolhardy Arab had popped into sight. An M-16 rained molten hell on Encizo and Katzenelenbogen. Almost indifferently then, Keio raised his own M-16 and caught the enemy on his blind side. A burst of four exploded the terrorman's head like a cantaloupe, blood and pulp splattering in runny streams all over the steel cowling.

There was respite. A silence swept over the *Beaumont*'s decks.

In hoarse authoritative tones, Yakov Katzenelenbogen called to the survivors in the bridgehouse. He used a perfectly enunciated Cairo dialect, universally understood in the Arab world: *"Esmah, ya binei miyye wa maya sharamit,"* he roared. "Listen, you sons of a hundred whores. You have a chance to live, even though you don't deserve it. We will give you sixty seconds to come out. Otherwise you all die."

A crudely bandaged head slowly appeared in the window, framed in jagged glass. Though Phoenix Force could not have known it, this was Emida Sarafid, right-hand man of Janda Yamani.

Sarafid sneered defiantly down at Yak.

"Save your breath, *Jehudi* scum," he taunted,

alternating between English and Arabic. "Ours is a holy war; we die with honor. *Kulshi min Allah.* We are ready to die. Are you?" Sarafid's M-16 suddenly swung up, spewed its deadly issue into the deck only inches to Katz's right. "Here's our answer," the terrorist screamed. "Here is our surrender!"

The night exploded anew, the fusillade now spinning off the bulwarks and deck, banging aloud in the bulkheads, hammering the steel gun mount shield, driving Encizo and Katzenelenbogen to cover. Yak did a swift dance in the alcove where he hid, actually felt a slug crease one rubber-coated leg—its kiss was hot, sobering.

Gary and Keio raised their submachine guns to return fire. But already Sarafid was down, cowering tight to the wall, his head likely between his knees.

Rafael called from his perch. "I'll work my way forward! Come around from behind them."

"No time," yelled Yak. "Got to get to the engineroom people. God knows what they've done to those poor sailors down there."

Quickly Katz scuttled around the stack, crabbed his way to where Keio was hugging steel. "The grenade launcher, Ohara," he snapped. "Slap it on. Lob some up into that bridgehouse. Let's get it over fast."

Keio groped into his duffel and drew out the M-203 grenade launcher attachment. He feverishly attached it to his M-16.

"Just get one inside," Katz encouraged. "That's all it will take."

Yak raised his Uzi, banged a short burst against the armor plate to keep any Arabs down, had to shove a fresh magazine into place.

Sight latch adjusted, Keio lined the launcher up with the forward leaf sight and triggered off the propelling round. As the M-16 roared, the M-26 grenade sped upward. "Shit!" he cursed as the wind-caught grenade went high, hit the flying bridge, bounced off into the ocean, exploded harmlessly just above waterline. A muffled pop carried from their right.

"There goes our little rubber yacht," Encizo laughed.

The second grenade landed low and bounced into the deck immediately to the front of the bridge doors. A fiery red mushroom, a metallic WHUMP, the rattle of shrapnel. But no cigar.

Keio again pumped in a cartridge, and the third projectile went up. This time it arced perfectly, hit the casement, bounced into the shack.

A babble of panic-stricken voices carried down as the Jeddahs decided whether to scoop up the uninvited visitor and toss it out.

One desperate Arab meanwhile took his chances on the door. What McCarter's AK-47 did not do to the front of him, the exploding grenade did to the back of him.

The man flung his blazing arms up to the sky as the concussion flung him off the bridge. He landed on the deck with a damp thump, full of holes, already half bled to death.

All weapons went silent again. The sudden pause of warfare was eerie once more. Up on the bridge there were no gurgling moans, nothing. Another minute passed before Katz said, "Up you go, Ohara. See what we've got."

As Keio loped toward the ladder that led to the

bridge, Yak and Manning peppered the shack with a half dozen slugs, just in case of survivors.

Keio topped the steel rungs, crawled around the bridge superstructure, AutoMag preceding him. He peered in through the blown-away door.

He winced, felt fleeting nausea at the definitive demonstration of what a grenade taken in closed quarters can do to a human body. The compartment was awash with slow-slithering blood; the walls were darkly splattered, pieces of cartilage and entrails clinging everywhere.

Sarafid and one other last-ditch hardman were all that was recognizably left, both lying in crumpled disarray. The lower part of Sarafid's face was gone, but his eyes were still wide with last-moment terror. His henchman had hands buried deep into his middle, fingers fighting to stuff his guts back into place even as he had died. Blood ran from his mouth and ears.

Keio quickly regained control and hurried to the side entry. His feet slid on the bloody steel. The sweetish smell of blood intermixed with the stench of voided excrement hit him head-on. He entered the abattoir, assessed the situation, and made sure he had missed nothing.

"Two that I can recognize," he called down to Yak.

"Eight gone for sure, then," Katzenelenbogen announced grimly as Keio returned. "So, the engine rooms!"

12

Encizo was left topside; the rest of the Phoenix assault force hurried to the portside engine room and started down the ladder. Manning took the lead.

There was no point in talking, for the thunder of the diesels drowned out all sound. Hand signals therefore, Keio following Gary, then David. Yak dropped off at the second deck and covered them against interior attack.

Manning felt sudden relief as he worked down the ladder, saw the three Americans still standing at their stations, just as he had left them. The Arabs were nowhere in sight. Which meant they had gone above and were now dead. Or else they had found a hiding place in the depths of the engine room, and were waiting in ambush.

The sailors beneath Gary were frozen robots, oblivious to his presence. There was no point in listening for movement, for giveaway vibrations; the engines obliterated that. There was only one way: frontal confrontation.

Gary eased off the safety catch on his Ingram MAC-10 and rechecked the magazine. He took a deep breath and dropped the final five feet into the engine room.

Instantly he spun, flopping onto the greasy deck,

feeling an icy knot in his gut in expectation of hot lead stitching his chest. A thump behind him caused him to whirl, but it was only Keio, carbon-copying his move, M-16 at ready, heading aft into the engine room.

Manning inched forward on his belly, cautiously exploring the maze of boilers and pipes crammed into the compartment. Shortly he dared rise to his knees, then into a laborious crouch. It was evident that the Arab overseers were long gone.

He returned to the hatch area to find Keio and David in tense huddle behind the crewmen.

Keio shouted into Gary's ear: "Our men have checked out for sure."

Even as Gary cocked his head to hear, David siezed the initiative and approached the Americans at the controls. "Full stop, sailor!" he roared, replaying his expedient action at Red Bluff. "Bring the ship to a full stop!"

The strong tone of command once more cut through drugged torpor. The three seamen mechanically commenced to flip switches, adjust gauges, pull control levers. Almost immediately the clamor in the torture box diminished. The engines fell to a relatively silent grumbling.

But the sailors heard no change. Once the orders were obeyed, they sank back into their trancelike state.

"Manning? Ohara?" Katz called down. "All okay?"

"Nobody's hurt down here. Our Arab buddies split," responded Gary.

"Up, then. We have to hit the aft engine room."

The jaw-clenched quartet worked its way aft

through the innards of the *Beaumont*, on guard every step that they took through the subterranean gloom.

They were only halfway down the ladder that led to the second engine room when they saw the lifeless tangle of bodies at its base.

Huge holes gaped in each man's head where the brains had been blown away at point-blank range.

Manning reacted the fastest. Scrambling the rest of the way down the ladder, he paused at the deck level, crouched and swiftly flung three grenades into the opening fore and aft, one of them deliberately lofted high for concussive effect.

The compartment blazed into blinding light. WHUMP-WHUMP-WHUMP.

There followed the staccato whistle and clatter of shrapnel as it dissected every cubic foot of the engine room.

After brief pause, Gary plummeted into the room, the Ingram MAC-10 already chattering, spraying the depths of the steel labyrinth. The racket was stunningly loud.

Then McCarter was beside him. Back-to-back they poured a dozen more rounds into the corners of the compartment. But it was mere vainglory; they were shooting at empty shadows.

"Gone," David muttered. His lips curled back over his teeth to transform his face into a death's head. "Good enough. Gives me time to get my own personal hands on 'em."

McCarter mimicked the actions of the crewmen in the port-engine room. Within ninety seconds the engines were turned down; the *Beaumont* would drift aimlessly from here on in.

The three men rejoined Katzenelenbogen on the second deck. Ashen-faced, they reported their foul finding.

"Okay," Yak said coolly. "They're holed up somewhere between here and the fantail. We start working our way back. Ohara, you go topside. Fill Encizo in on what's happening. Tell him to rotate between the two berthing areas. Then you go aft, station yourself above the screws in case we flush either of them abovedecks. Everybody—kneecap them if you can. We need some talk real bad."

There was time for each man to replace empty, half-empty magazines and to reposition remaining ammo. There was time for pulses to moderate somewhat, for the dangerous vengeance haze to drift away from behind each man's eyes.

Now the trio moved forward in the half-darkness, warily, freezing often to listen for betraying sounds. The *Beaumont* was slowing, and the increased wallow and pitch made footing precarious. The muted engines allowed each creak of over-aged steel and rivets to sound that much more pronounced.

An assortment of approximately thirty packing crates in a staging area took them ten minutes to work through. Next they came upon machine shops, welding and at-sea repair rooms. Side excursions were made into storage compartments that branched off of each shop area.

"We're getting a bit far back," Yak murmured. "If we don't flush them soon, we'll have to go down into the magazines."

Business picked up as they reached the fantail.

They were approaching the after-steering compartment where the auxiliary hydraulic units provided steering backup, should the *Beaumont* sustain wartime damage to its primary steering controls. As the three mercenaries padded softly toward the area they encountered the only connecting passageway. There they were brought to a dead stop by a muffled cough.

It came from inside the after-steering compartment.

McCarter motioned the others back.

"A live one," he whispered. All froze, intently listening. There was no further sound.

"Well?" David silently mouthed at Katz.

"Alive," Katz said softly. "Gary, you hang back, don't make a sound," he continued in faint whisper. "David, you and I, we'll walk on by, go topside... make them think we've overlooked them. Gary, you play possum until they think they're safe and sneak out on their own. You cover down here...coldcock them if you possibly can...."

Manning nodded.

Katz and David loudly thumped through the abbreviated passageway, slammed doors on attached storage bins, talked openly. They held fake confab at the base of the ladder to the upper deck. "Nobody here," McCarter blustered. "Let's look topside, boss."

They made a big production of coming out of the hatch abovedecks, moved in the direction of the bow, motioned to Keio en route—he was crouched behind tarpaulin-shrouded cargo—to *stay put*.

They stomped noisily to midships, then carefully doubled back to the fantail, and crouched down to wait.

Ten minutes later their silent vigil paid off. With a sibilant squeak, the after-steering compartment hatch began to rise. All hands ducked back. Phoenix Force huddled in the muffling darkness.

The hatch opened halfway, then stopped. A dusky face peered out. He muttered something to the man below, then started out. Standing on point, his M-16 roving the entire fantail, he waited until his vision adapted while his companion came abovedecks.

With a soft click the hatch was dropped and the duo started forward.

Keio floated up from his hiding place, took three swift steps toward the Arab in the rear, his right hand came up, it sliced down with deadly speed. The Nukite palm strike at the base of his skull connected solidly. The victim jerked with white-out pain, went down like a brain-shot ox.

Keio caught the body in midair. He sought to wrap his arms around both the Arab and his weapon so as not to warn his advance man. But the M-16 twirled on its strap, the butt clanged the deck hard, and the noise caused his comrade to wheel.

Reflexively, Keio fell away, left the body virtually hanging in midair.

The point man in panic raised his M-16 and shot. The bullets spewed into his buddy's belly, ripped him apart.

McCarter flung himself at the stunned assassin and sent him sprawling on the deck. The gunman's M-16 shot more flame into empty air, then the released weapon cartwheeled across the steel deck.

The Arab fought to recover the weapon, twisting savagely to shake off his attacker.

David McCarter grabbed the Arab by the hair and commenced to methodically hammer his head against the deck.

He was still hammering when Yak caught him from behind, dragged him away. Encizo and Manning, coming from opposite directions, closed in at the same time, helped him pull McCarter off.

"Cool it, David," Katz commanded. "We want him alive."

Keio had wrestled the Arab up off the deck, now held him in a full nelson, bending the man's body halfway over.

Yak advanced on him. He gripped the terrorist's nose between the steel hooks of his prosthesis, applying near-amputating pressure as he dragged the man's head up.

"Talk!" Katz spat in Arabic. "Where are the rest of your friends? Where'd they go? Where have you hidden the guns?"

The Arab tried to twist away from Katz's bizarre hold, squealed. Blood dripped from his gashed forehead, from his nose. "I don't know!" he screamed in his native tongue. "I am a soldier, I take orders. I am not informed...."

"You lie!" Yak then motioned to Keio. "Let him go."

The Arab swayed. He almost fell. Yak smashed him across the side of the face with his metal hand. The guy staggered.

"Talk, you bastard. While you have a chance." He grinned malevolently. "Or would you rather I turned you over to him...." He indicated the wild-eyed McCarter, then the stony-faced Ohara "...or him? They'll kill you by inches."

"Master, I do not know. I am but a mere...."

Yak waved David forward. With a grating snarl, as if wishing to expend all his bubbling hatred in one swift stroke, McCarter brought up a haymaker that nearly tore the man's head off.

The guy screamed, still fought to escape in maddened despair, but Ohara braced him and powerfully flung him back at David. *"Effendi, effendi..."* the man drooled, his lower teeth wiped out, "...I know nothing. I...."

Again McCarter bore in, landed a punishing right to his stomach, his hand disappearing in the Arab's gut. The hardman screamed, gagged, doubled over.

McCarter moved in for another shot but Yak waved him off. "Don't be greedy, David. Give somebody else a chance."

When the Jeddah murderer could get his breath again, Encizo stepped forward and drove his fist into the man's nose. It was a politely executed maneuver, but it viciously crunched the nose flat in one blow. The Arab squealed like a shock victim. He tried to roll into a ball of cowering flesh on the deck, but Yak held him upright.

"The guns," Yak said. "The rest of your strike force. Where are they?"

"I swear I do not know...."

The rest of it was bloody and brutal.

"Enough!" Yak finally roared, stopping the gory mayhem.

The Jeddah hardman had not been taught about the mind-bending, endless pain, about these men with murder in their hands. His leaders had neglected to forewarn him about a force such as Phoenix Force.

And then, after several minutes, during which he had hawked up blood, spat it along with bits of flesh and spare teeth onto the deck—even through mangled teeth, fractured jaw, broken nose—the Arab suddenly mocked them, spoke in perfect English, with a twisted, broken smile: "They are gone, *Jehudi*," he hissed. "The guns are gone. The submarine took them away to Libya!"

For long moments there was no sound. The whistle of the wind, the rattle of rain on rubber suits seemed suddenly loud.

The weapons gone?

All those helpless American military killed . . . for what?

McCarter was the first to react. He charged the sneering terrorist once more, fists flailing insanely. It was berserk time.

David's last blow landed squarely on the guy's Adam's apple, snapping a vital cord in his larynx. The man coughed hideously, clawed desperately at his throat. Before the eyes of Phoenix Force, his face turned blue. A shrill sound tore through his ruptured epiglottis, and he sagged.

Keio came behind him, applied pressure to his ribs in hard, rhythmic clenchings. McCarter stumbled away, his expression dazed, realizing—too late—his deadly error.

Keio's efforts were futile. The man was dead; the critical timetable had gone with him. Finally Keio relaxed his grip, and the Arab fell onto the deck, his face sliding in his own blood.

13

Upon being shuttled back to the *Dauntless*, Colonel Katzenelenbogen closeted himself in the radio shack, and did not emerge for two hours. Stony Man, when apprised of latest developments, immediately tied in to Fleet Command Center lines in Norfolk, Virginia and Washington, D.C. Brognola recontacted at 0330 hours, informing Yak that the message had been relayed; ASWCCCS was now alerted.

At the U.S. Navy Anti-Submarine Warfare Center Command and Control System, a C3 alert was posted on war boards at NATO Tactical Command and at Acoustic Research Center in California. At Acoustic the massive computer banks were prepped and put on standby. OSIS—Ocean Surveillance Information System—which was affiliated with ASWCCCS, was also notified.

"The entire naval ASW system's on call," Hal Brognola reported. "Two pursuit subs are under way. They'll be employing dunking sonar, sonobuoys, Barra-type thermal detecting, the whole galaxy. They'll have that sector of the Atlantic covered like a blanket by noon."

Katz sighed wearily, drained by the high-level tensions under which Phoenix had been operating these past ninety-six hours. "Whatever happened to the good old days when you came on hand-to-hand, Hal?''

Bolan's "head fed" laughed. "They're still with us, buddy. You'll get a bellyful before this caper's wrapped up, believe me."

"We want Ghazawi... we want blood."

"Listen up, Yak. The *Nimitz* has been designated as a control center. You must maintain close liaison between them and the *Dauntless*. Your contact is a Lieutenant Commander Aspinall—he's under orders to cooperate one hundred percent. They'll quartermaster anything the *Dauntless* can't dig up. They'll be putting up every loose chopper they've got—they have some Sikorsky Sea Kings that are the hottest thing going—they'll launch a dozen Grumman Trackers to provide additional MAD cover. In other words, my friend, they guarantee a pinpoint for you by sundown.... You sound beat, Katz. I think it's time you got some shut-eye. Mighty big day tomorrow. Today, I mean."

Sack time was brutally abbreviated. Three-plus hours later, at 0700 hours, dawn hardly broken, Katz was routing his men from their bunks. "Breakfast, gentlemen!" he called. "We don't want to keep the whole Second Fleet waiting."

Yak briefed them on individual detection sorties that each would be involved in throughout the day, computer-devised by Stony Man. "Then," he concluded, "I have a suspicion that we will be doing a little underwater duty ourselves before the world is another twenty-four hours older. Sound like fun?"

"Definitely," Manning said, serious to the last.

"Deal me in," Davey nodded. "We'll make the old Atlantic run red, won't we?"

The weather was still foul, a steady rain fell, the wind blustered out of the northeast at a brisk ten knots.

The temperature stood at forty-four degrees. "A beautiful day for some execution," muttered McCarter. Phoenix Force piled into the copter and prepared to be relayed to the *Nimitz*, standing due east, fifteen miles off.

In an O-1 wardroom, they were introduced to Craig Aspinall, a lean, gray-eyed officer who greeted them with an austere smile, then immediately got down to business.

On a huge plot-board, his staff had already broken the Atlantic between the *Nimitz* and Gibraltar into precise grids, each segment encompassing two hundred square knots. "We have a dozen helicopters aloft. Two of you will ride shotgun on some Sikorsky HSS-2s. The rest will be in Grummans. They will fly the outer limits of our parameter."

Aspinall explained that expert estimates had placed the Arab sub's maximum lead on them at five to six hundred knots. "We suspect they're running in a Soviet castoff, which would have a top underwater speed of twenty knots. Allowing them a twenty-four hour head start, they'd still be in striking range. We'll crisscross this five-hundred knot grid here with everything we've got."

"And when we find the sub?" Yak said, his eyes cool, receptive.

"My orders state that we somehow force them to

surface. Destruction of the sub, loss of the war material is the last possible alternative action." He stared at Yak. "I guess you have experience with things like that."

"I guess we soon will."

Phoenix Force was on the landing deck, boarding separate aircraft. Yak, Encizo and Manning climbed into Grumman S2F-1 Trackers. McCarter and Ohara strapped into Sea King harnesses. "Happy hunting," David yelled at the last, sending cocky thumbs-up to everyone as his Sikorsky HSS-2 lifted off the deck.

On their way to the farthest edge of the search quadrant, the Tracker's copilot explained to Rafael—the magnetic airborne detector (MAD)—a six-foot-long spar extending from the craft's underbelly. "We skim the ocean at about thirty feet," he said. "The MAD can locate a submarine no matter what the depth, by homing in on the magnetic field of its submerged mass. Once it registers on the gauges, we simply figure the coordinates and we're in business. In war conditions we'd call in a missile strike, or drop depth charges...but I hear you don't exactly want to blow this one out of the water."

"No, we have other plans," Encizo said.

While the Grummans crisscrossed their assigned grid with tedious precision, each pass one hundred feet inside the last one, the whirlybirds employed a different method of detection. Hovering close to the surface, the Sea Kings—ASW workhorses carrying electronics equal to a frigate, plus anti-sub torpedoes—lowered a sonar head five feet into the ocean. Complex electronics registered the magnetics, vibration and noise of any submarine within range. If the sonar detected nothing, the device was raised and dunked in another spot down the line.

And when the submarine was finally detected? Immediate imprint of its engine noise, of its displacement in the ocean depths, would be transmitted via satellite to the Acoustic Research Center. Here the computers would automatically switch into a tape library in which recordings of underwater engine noise of every submarine currently in service were stored. Instantaneous identification of the sub, its complement and firepower, would flash to Fleet Command, then to OSIS and ASWCCCS, packet-switched to all relevant command posts in seconds. From that moment on, the sub in question would be thrown into jeopardy. Deadly jeopardy; its moments would be numbered.

The day seemed endless, each man chafing in his observer role, having no direct hand in apprehending the phantom sub.

When in hell were those beepers going to sing?

As it turned out, they were denied even that small victory... for at 1530 hours a crisp communication from the *Nimitz* broke the silence. "Target has been identified," the radio crackled. "All auxiliary aircraft return to base."

"Sheeeit," David swore in his seat aboard the HSS-2. "Are you guys *sure* you had that dunk gadget turned on? A dry run, is that all we get?"

The Trackers wheeled, clawed for altitude, sped for home. Katz, Encizo and Manning were already in the briefing room, hot coffee and sandwiches before them, when David and Keio trotted in—their sluggish copters had been the last vehicles the LSO waved aboard.

The printout was in hand. "It's a Russian diesel," Katz said finally, when the mess-boy had gone and David and Keio had downed their first swig of reviving java. "A real relic. It's a particularly messy modification in the whisky twin-cylinder class. She cruises at ten knots submerged, fifteen surfaced. Can you believe that? She carries a regular complement of fifty-six, and has six torpedo tubes, two missile tubs. More than likely it's unarmed this mission. They claim she sounds like a freight train on the sonar."

"Where'd they find it?" Keio asked.

"Aspinall overestimated on speed. He never dreamed anyone would use a tub like this. It's only two hundred eighty miles on its way. Found it at thirty-eight degrees, thirty minutes north; eighteen degrees, nineteen minutes west. Too far south to be heading for Gibraltar. Looks like they're set to unload somewhere off the coast of Morocco."

"What now?" Encizo challenged.

"The navy will put three copters on it, round-the-clock. At least until we're ready to make our move."

"Which is?"

"My, Rafael," Yak smiled indulgently, "you ask so many hard questions." He took a swallow of coffee. "We wait on further orders, that's what. I, for one, need some sleep. Maybe we can take in the nightlife aboard the *Nimitz*. See a movie, play some pool. Exciting stuff like that."

"Level with us, *compadre*," Encizo insisted. "What do *you* think we're gonna do?"

"You heard the options this morning, Rafael. We

have to figure a way to force them to surface before they reach their rendezvous.''

"Why not trail them to Morocco?" Keio asked. "They have to come up sometime. Then we nail them.''

"Oh? You think Khadaffi won't have an aerial and seaborne strike force standing by? That means open war of sorts, doesn't it, if we attack them? Remember—no newspapers, and save those DSLGs. This is a Sensitive Mission. And, too, maybe it's a way for me to get my hands on Ghazawi. . . .''

14

It was Thursday, October 28; ten days had passed since Phoenix Force first received notice to scramble in El Paso.

It was the beginning of the team's sixth day at sea.

Small wonder tensions ran high, that each man was honed to wire-edge, that their attention wandered during the all-morning briefings that Phoenix Force sat through aboard the *Nimitz* as submarine experts, diving experts, demolition experts paraded in steady stream through the briefing room.

Time was getting away from them. They'd be old men before they saw the end of the damnable Jeddah caper!

Blood. Terrorist blood. *It must be had.*

The *Nimitz* was standing by, keeping a careful twenty knots behind the sub to lull the Russki's Tamir sonar devices. The *Dauntless*, steaming at ten knots, held a course twenty miles ahead of it. In between the two ships, the Sikorsky HSS-2s kept unceasing vigil.

Katz and his men prepared for any and all exigencies. Supplied with telephoto schematics from the CIA, each knew both the outer configurations and the inner layout of the Russian sub like the back of his hand. Each man knew where and how, and with which weapons, to ferret out every last Arab maggot skulking within its labyrinthine guts.

In the books, the unwieldy piece of Russian junk originally constructed in the 1950s was classified as cruise missile submarine SSG, twin-cylinder class. It was two hundred fifty feet long. Its snubbed conning tower was built directly at midships, so that it resembled a squat black slug. Just aft of the sail area, protected by an angular steel fairing, lay the twin missile silos—placed like laid-down whisky bottles, thus the cavalier classification. When raised to proper angle by clumsy hydraulics, an SS N 3A Soviet missile could be fired from each. Additional armament consisted of twelve 553mm torpedoes which could be fired from torpedo rooms located fore and aft.

While it boasted two diesel electric engines, plus various electrical auxiliaries, and was listed as having a thirteen-thousand-mile range, the monstrosity had not once, in its nonillustrious history, ever come close to these outer limits. Plagued by eternal mechanical breakdowns, also by a succession of Ivan Potato deck officers who could not begin to find their collective asses with both hands, the class had become an outright embarrassment to the Russian Navy.

Even though modified in succeeding versions that appeared in the late fifties and early sixties, the whisky class never achieved its potential, and was eventually relegated to mere submarine trainer status.

At least until they found someone dumb enough to take these underwater disasters off their hands. Enter

Muammar the Dull, who was not particularly known as a shrewd bargainer. It goes bang, I buy, was Khaddafi's motto.

"I doubt that there are any missiles aboard," Katzenelenbogen said as they neared the end of the briefing on the sub's external details. "Most likely the silos are sealed empty to save weight for transport of the contraband. They might even have the weapons stored inside the silos," he said in afterthought, "but I would doubt that."

"And how do we crack this tin can?" asked McCarter.

"As I say, we have to find a way to make those cutthroats surface."

All knew that the Stony Man computer-devised strategy called for immediate dispatch of U.S. subs from the Gibraltar area. But the subs were still thirty-six hours away from the *Nimitz*. Even after the deadly fighter submarines arrived, there was still no clear-cut plan for their utilization. Thus the need for interim strategies became more pressing with each passing hour. The U.S. subs *Tullibee* and the *Sea Wolf* could discharge their MK-64 torpedoes and put that double stovepipe to the bottom at any time.

But that, of course, was no way to bring Jeddah up for a sunning.

For a time then, at the instigation of Rafael, they discussed the U.S. Navy's deep submergence rescue vehicles (DSRVs), developed for the purpose of bringing up trapped submariners. Two of these were operational, had cost Uncle Sam roughly sixty-five million dollars to build.

"In the first place," Aspinall demurred, "it's

altogether too risky to attempt dropping an underwater assault team at those depths. Even as slow as
the Russian submarine is, it is still inconceivable that
any divers would be so skillful—or so lucky—as to
clamp onto a sub moving underwater at ten knots.''

Encizo bristled at this. ''Hey, I've had much training in underwater demolition. I can't begin to count
the hours I've spent in actual salvage operations.''

''Even so,'' Aspinall countered, ''the fact that the
Jeddah technicians will more than likely pick up the
vehicle on their sonar is a serious consideration. If
they do, they will act more quickly, take faster evasive diving action, than a DSRV can—and there goes
the mission. Then too, the DSRVs must be delivered
to the indicated depth via a piggyback harness that is
available only on specially equipped submarines.
And we don't have any of those subs closer than the
Boston navy yard.''

Rafael shrugged. ''Well, it was just a thought.''

But how valuable that thought truly became evident only when the wardroom skull session was
reconvened after lunch, and the nagging question—
how to board the sub while it still ran underwater—
continued to haunt them.

By that time Encizo had done his homework
aboard the *Nimitz*. He began to describe a more ple-
bian frogman device called the Sea Horse II discovered on his explorations beneath the landing deck,
which was a swimmer-delivery vehicle designed to
transport naval underwater teams in shallower
depths. Eyes opened wider, pulse rates revved.

''Well, underwater expert,'' Yak finally confronted Rafael head-on. ''Is it within the faintest realm of
possibility?''

"At least we have one of the things, so I say yes, it is," Encizo said, a thoughtful expression furrowing his face. "Just barely. We'll need ten percent skill and ninety percent luck to pull it off. The timing would have to be pinpoint perfect."

Yak's eyes were grave. "Are you and Manning willing to try? If there's every chance that you won't come out alive, that's a hell of a thing to ask."

"I was never big on old-age benefits," Rafael replied.

"Gary?"

"I'm in." Manning's face was impassive. "Who else knows explosives as well as I do?"

"Okay, let's talk some more."

What Phoenix Force talked about were the nitty-gritty technologies involved in the care and feeding of a diesel submarine. They all understood that Ivan's sub could remain underwater a maximum of fifty to sixty hours before having to recharge its storage batteries and continue its cruise. Under normal conditions the sub would surface, then float for twelve hours while the diesels were cranked up and batteries given fresh zap. But during wartime and emergency conditions, the sub could recharge by snorkeling. Cruising at twenty to twenty-five feet beneath the surface, it would poke its snorkel tube up, draw oxygen, expel diesel smoke discreetly.

When a sub snorkels, however, it becomes vulnerable in another way. Because of water pressure against the snorkel while the sub is moving, leaks pose a serious threat. Therefore the sub must reduce speed—to four and five knots—to minimize this danger. In the case of the Russian whisky class, this speed could likely be even less, perhaps three, even two knots per hour.

The Jeddah force had been cruising at two hundred feet for at least thirty-six hours now; it *must* come up for recharge sometime within the next twenty-four hours or face disaster. Since the Sea King crewmen had reported no depth-level change since the beginning of their vigil, the surfacing was overdue. The moment their detection devices registered such a change, word would flash to the *Nimitz*. From there to the *Dauntless*. And thus to Phoenix Force.

A scuba team would never be able to attach itself to a sub moving at ten knots, or even five knots. But with luck, with its placement just right, a scuba duo delivered underwater by a Sea Horse SDV could board a sub moving at two or three knots. It could tie on to exterior cleats, rails or sail ladders....

This was the life-and-death assignment Encizo and Manning had chosen to accept.

"There has to be a carbon dioxide level buildup starting already down there," Encizo mused. "Their scrubbers can't do it forever."

"Okay," said Manning, "so we manage to latch on. Then what?"

"We immobilize the sub."

"How?"

"We attach charges to the screws, blow 'em clean off."

"Wouldn't they just close the rear hatches and sink to the bottom again? So we'd be back at square one?"

"Not if that Arab captain knows anything at all.

Without screws they can't maneuver. Without air they'll die. Their batteries are almost shot, remember. Without power they can't even blow their tubes to resurface. It's a total checkmate. Surfacing is the only option they have left.''

Thus it was decided.

Phoenix went on nonstop alert, starting immediately.

All afternoon, all hands kept an eye on the door of the radio shack on O-2, waiting for word that the Arabs were finally beginning snorkeling procedures. Tension heightened with each passing hour. The wind came up; the weather thickened; the day began to fade. And still no word.

To a man they pitied the sorry sons of bitches who'd have to climb into wet suits, load aboard that swimmer-delivery vehicle, be dunked into the icy Atlantic—in the middle of a freezing, end-of-October night!

Though he was an ex-Catholic, and held hard cynical views about religion, Rafael Encizo was forced to agree with Mack Bolan that if you were on the right side, the universe would unfold as it should...for at precisely 0620 hours—dawn a pewter smudge on the horizon—the alert came. Not in the dark of night, but on the verge of crystalline-bright new day!

Jeddah had finally had enough of recirculating its own farts. They were on their way up.

He and Manning struggled into their just-doused exposure suits, then attached their double tanks. Side by side they broke out onto the barren deck, hunched against a rising wind, and strapped themselves into the SDV's open cockpit. The baby tornado set up by the transport copter's rotors chilled them further, made them gasp for breath. They checked their demolition supplies for the tenth time. The copter rose from the deck and hovered above them.

Now the lifting harness was slowly lowered, and Rafael and Gary swiftly snapped the large clevis hooks into the Sea Horse II's loading rings.

A minute later they were slowly lifting off the deck. Below them they saw Yak, Keio and David waving at them, figures that rapidly got smaller and smaller.

Encizo doggedly ran the submarine's coordinates through his mind—Katz's last communication just before Rafael had climbed into the SDV.

It seemed like only moments had passed when they felt the copter slack off, felt the SDV rock in its harness.

As soon as zero stability was achieved, the whirly-bird began settling down. The cable sang, lowering them in fits and starts. Sixty seconds later, they were down.

They unsnapped the hooks and the vehicle, like an elongated fiberglass pickle, wallowed on the ocean swells. The electric motor, powered by a forty-eight volt lead-acid battery, capable of pushing the SDV at three knots submerged, instantly thrummed to life.

They headed for the advancing submarine.

Trim procedures had been seen to on the previous day; Sea Horse II was dive-ready. Still, dreading the first savage shock of the icy water, Encizo dallied. "Ready, Gary?" he called, just before inserting his mouthpiece. "Last chance to change your mind."

"Put her down, you bastard!" Manning smiled, bracing for the ripping onslaught himself. "Let's get it over with!"

Encizo sent him a last grin, demonic challenge to it, and repeated the coordinates one last time. "Fathometer setting will be fifteen feet. Help keep me on target." A last adjustment of his face mask, a tug on his rubber hood, and then the mouthpiece went in. No more talking. Hand signals from here on.

The buoyancy chamber began to blow. Encizo pushed the control stick forward. The vehicle slowly dived. Even though the cold slammed him like a monstrous fist, made his guts constrict, Rafael remembered yesterday's drills and moved the SDV smoothly into the water at moderate angle. No hurry; thirty minutes remained before they crossed paths with the sub.

Then they were under, totally submerged, the pain of the cold a shrieking mistral in his brain. Encizo writhed in his seat, fought for sanity. He would never get used to this sensation of driving a boat underwater, the current buffeting his body, twisting his head every foot of the way. Meanwhile Manning, though inexperienced in aquatic activities, would stoically withstand any amount of chill and pain.

It was murky under the surface, visibility poor even at ten feet. Hopefully, when the sun rose, things would improve. Rafael held the control lever forward, dug five feet deeper into the ocean, then leveled off. He groaned with relief as his body gradually became accustomed to the cold, the exposure suit magically activating thermal kickback. Even brick-built Manning would be relieved at the change.

Rafael looked sideways, got a nodding smile from around Manning's mouthpiece.

The Sea Horse plowed steadily on. The small turbulence that its prop kicked up carried faintly Rafael's eyes flitted from the gauges to the undulating dark shimmerings in the water before him, back to the gauges again, as he fought to keep the flimsy craft on course. Tension mounted as Encizo thought about losing the sub... it could pass a quarter of a mile away from them and they wouldn't see it in this underwater hell. Even if the vibration of the screws alerted him, it would already be too late; the SDV could never catch up once the sub got past them.

Anxiety built as fifteen, then twenty minutes passed. Now twenty-five minutes. And still no sight of that damned Russian tin can!

Suddenly his heart exploded with adrenaline. Off to the right, coming head-on—

He gasped at the size of the underwater monster, at the speed—even at three knots—that it was traveling. The sub was twenty-four feet wide at the sail area. Its sail structure loomed a full twenty feet above the main hull, and even a fleeting glance verified that its periscope, as well as the ESM mast and the snorkel, were up—all doing their thing. The missile tubes, flat on the deck behind the sail bulwarks, were enormous. Great black silos, forty feet long, sturdily capped on each end against the time that they would be elevated and fired.

No time for further appraisal of the enemy. Rafael and Gary were clipping equipment to their belts, looping drift ropes around their shoulders. The light was better now. They took precise fix on the sail tower's boarding ladder, gauging the distance on a second-to-second basis.

As they had practiced repeatedly the day before, the two warriors prepared to leave the SDV while it was still at a safe distance from the sub. It would not do for the sub to bang into it. Deftly Rafael set the controls, put the vehicle at neutral buoyancy, turned the wheel sharply to the left, and sent it scooting away from the approaching behemoth.

The SDV would lose power in another two hours; the Sea Kings would eventually find it and drop frogmen to recover it.

Encizo signaled to Manning and they set off for the submarine, now a hundred and fifty feet away and bearing down on them with intimidating speed. Their hearts hammered as they came alongside, felt the sucking current that enveloped the massive hull, a current that could propel them down the sides of the sub and into the screws themselves, to be churned to a bloody puree.

They kicked harder, came within ten feet of the sail area—human gnats assaulting an unsuspecting giant—their hands outstretched, groping for the boarding ladder: Encizo high, Manning low.

Fingers clamped on the rungs, legs jammed behind the ladder.

They rested, their breathing resounding in their masks.

Then Encizo sent Manning an over-the-top signal and began working his way across the conning tower with slow, deliberate care. A moment later he was out of sight.

Manning knew exactly what he must do next. Each move would be precise, mechanical, perfect.

The heavy drift rope was tied firmly to the ladder, the slide buckles unsorted from the two-hundred-foot coil. Now, playing out line foot by foot, his legs flailing to hold position, Gary floated back and drifted toward the propellers. The motion of the sub literally plastered his body to the hull.

On the other side of the submarine, Encizo was employing the same tactics, his line snugged to a huge bulwark cleat. The current grew more turbulent the farther back each man got.

Every foot brought them closer to possible disaster—death of the goriest sort. They were fifteen feet from the screws... ten feet.

The water became wilder, the noise of the pounding screws deafening, despite the decreasing speed. Each man engaged his line clamp now, the bites adjusted more precisely and painstakingly than ever; if the loops should slip now—

They moved closer, hands scrabbling for purchase on the scaly hull, each bite now a matter of six inches. Three feet... two feet....

The twin screws were within reach. Exact final adjustments were made in the line; the two men were now locked firmly at a distance where each could work on the elongated round housings, but not so close that his hands might inadvertently be sucked into the whirling screws.

Though their fingers ached, felt wooden from the chilling water, their intense concentration narcoticized pain. Each movement was deliberate as they produced sash cord and unloaded the MK-133 demoli-

tion haversack. Working in tandem, Gary handling
the explosives, Rafael tying them in place, his fingers
feeding cord from his belt with surgeonlike precision,
they placed four sticks on each screw housing. When
set off by a time-delay detonator, they would easily
shear the props, put a kink in the screw shafts as well.

The hull rivets would also pop in a radius of four
to six feet, causing multiple leaks that could not be
ignored. But most critical was the sub's helplessness
once its screws were gone. There would be no alternative: surface. Either that or drown like rats in a
barrel.

As they worked, each avenger was careful about
noise. There must be no telltale clank of tools on
steel, no thump of air tanks on the plates. Should the
Arab listening devices alert them to the impending
sabotage, they would simply rev up the screws—and
dive. The mere thought gave each man a constant
grinding sensation in the pit of the stomach.

Manning would have preferred to wrap plastic explosive around each housing, but this might have
been more time consuming, more risky with the
screws churning inches away. Thus the MK-133s. A
cute little eight-pack of death, each block of MK 23
weighing two-and-a-half pounds....

What a happy pounding that would give the Russki
sub!

Five agonizing minutes later the task was done.
Encizo tightened the bindings a last notch; Manning
double-checked on the waterproofed detonator.
Thirty minutes: more than enough time to clear the
area. The trigger was activated. The death clock
ticked.

Slowly each man wheeled and took up firm slack on the line; this was no time to lose one's grip. They began working back, hand over hand, to the submarine's sail, exulting in the large muscle movements. They must disconnect then and lunge upward from the sail deck, to keep from being caught in the vortex and sucked, after all, into the screws.

The line was finally retrieved, coiled and draped around their chests. Next they climbed the ladder again and ducked down in the tower cowling to assess the strength of Russian steel. How much TNT would it take to blow that hatch, knock Jeddah on its collective ass long enough to blow the inner hatch as well?

Gary's eyes narrowed behind his face mask, charge estimates clicking in his brain.

At last Manning and Encizo rose from the deck with a fierce shove-off. They veered left from the sail and put quick distance between them and the sub. There was a distinct pull, but they counteracted it with savage fin kicks and were soon free of its influence. Smiling grimly, they paddled in place and watched the submarine fade sluggishly into the murk.

It was torture to remain beneath the water another fifteen minutes, but they endured it. If the Arab commander was at the periscope, he would certainly be alerted if he saw two froggies bob up in his wake.

Then it was time to surface. They exploded into blinding sunlight. They tore away their mouthpieces, howled at the top of their lungs—thankful to be alive!

Minutes later the fluorescent orange rescue panel was spread out between them, catching the morning sun like a fiery finger. A chopper, loafing at three hundred feet, perhaps two miles to the northeast, spun on its rotors and rattled toward them.

The pickup hook came down. Both got their foot in the stirrup and clung to the line. The winch whirred, and they were climbing into a glaringly blue sky. Encizo suppressed still another victorious whoop. Mission accomplished, goddamn.

"What is happening, my brother captain?" Janda Yamani said, standing in the background, where Khader Ghazawi hung on the shoulder of the sub commander, Khalid Haddad, as he peered anxiously into the periscope eyepiece. "What does he see?"

"Silence, fool!" Ghazawi spat. "How can anyone concentrate with your gabble?"

An eerie silence hung within the submarine. A twenty-five-man skeleton crew, plus the eighteen Jeddah terrorists, had been on edge since the snorkeling began.

Resentment was a sullenly burning ember among the regular submariners. They were loyal to Khadaffi, to Haddad, but not to this Jeddah lunatic. Could they not have waited another ten hours, snorkeled at sunset? But no. The Jeddah people had complained of headaches, lethargy caused by the bad air, so they were surfacing in broad daylight.

Bad air? This was nothing. They didn't know what bad air was. Whining women, that's what they were.

Thus the friction grew, with two separate camps formed. The crew sulked and slept in their quarters, avoiding Jeddah, manning duty stations with sullen haphazardness.

More likely than not, their snorkel wake would be

seen, they would be bombed at any moment. They would all die in this stinking steel coffin.

And all because of these filthy Jeddah misfits!

"There is aircraft perhaps," Haddad reported. "But at great distance. It is hard to tell whether they have discovered us, however. And our sonar is picking up distant shipping. Whether they are naval forces we cannot determine. I suggest that to be safe, we discontinue snorkeling. We must dive once more. The air has improved—we have enough power to cruise until nightfall—we can resume our recharge procedures then. . . ."

"No!" Ghazawi snarled. "We must continue as we are. Even if they do see us, the *Amrikani* will not destroy this submarine. You do not know how much these weapons mean to them."

"I am in command here," Haddad retorted angrily. "I say we go down."

"You forget, *ya akhui*," Ghazawi placated the man, "that I take my orders from Pasha Khaddafi also. By his authority my word supersedes yours. We will continue as we are."

Commander Haddad threw up his shoulders in surrender. He knew how irrational Khaddafi could be when he thought he was crossed. "All right, Ghazawi," he agreed. "But I predict disaster."

The decision, in the end, was neither man's to make. For less than ten minutes later—

Khader Ghazawi was in his compartment, haranguing Yamani over the miserable Yemeni dog's insolence, when the submarine was rocked by a dull double-barreled explosion. A heavy, rolling shudder swept the length of the sub. Instant pandemonium erupted, confused commands, screams carrying from the aft areas.

Captain Haddad was livid when Ghazawi broke into the command section. "You insufferable fool!" he choked. "See what you have done! An underwater team has come upon us unawares. They have destroyed our screws. We are without power. We are taking on water in the after compartments. We must surface!"

"No!" Ghazawi gasped, his face going white.

"We have no choice. We will all drown."

"Repair the damage, seal off the compartments!" Ghazawi thought of Colonel Yakov Katzenelenbogen, his fearless crew of gunfighters very large in his mind all at once. "Certainly there is something we can do. We must go to the bottom if necessary."

"Go to the bottom? *Are you mad?* With no power, no maneuverability? We would not come up again, my crazy friend. No, we must surface. We must surrender to the *Amrikani*. We will come to terms."

He whirled away from Ghazawi, began barking rapid, hysterical orders.

15

Encizo and Manning had shed their underwater gear immediately on being dropped onto the *Dauntless*.

Now, dressed in regular battle uniforms—camouflage jump suits and field caps, Yak's eternal black tam at jaunty angle—the entire Phoenix Force team sat inside the idling helicopter and waited for the Arab sub to blow.

0815 hours. The *Dauntless* had made a wide sweep even as Gary and Rafael had worked underwater; now it was only five miles to the southeast of the Russian whisky class. Once the death eggs exploded, Phoenix would be instantly airborne and marking the area before the sub even surfaced.

"Here she goes!" Encizo yelled as his watch's second hand touched 0821 hours. "Surprise, you murdering bastards!"

It wasn't that much of a show. They saw an angry, squat geyser spew water about twelve feet into the air. Then a muffled, disappointing rumble carried to them. A moment later the waves had moved back in, erasing the puny turbulence with one long swell as if nothing had happened.

"Think it did the job?" McCarter asked.

"How'd you like a bangalore shoved up *your* ass, mate?" Gary Manning muttered. "Think it'd make you blink?"

Fleeting vision of troops shooting at each other at Red Bluff Arsenal came to the collective mind of Phoenix—as did remembrance of the murdered Lockheed Starlifter crew...of the sailors they had watched helplessly executed on the *Beaumont*'s deck...and the pile of human garbage—their brains leaking out—that they had found in the *Beaumont*'s forward engine room less than five days ago.

"Go!" Katzenelenbogen roared, his heart soaring.

The pilot revved the engine and eagerly hit the stick. As the copter lifted off and executed a starboard slide, gaining altitude, Phoenix Force rechecked cartridge belts, weapons and ammo. Gary and Rafael feverishly lined up the dozen haversacks of explosives, fuses, detonators and demolition tools near the door.

The helicopter hovered at fifty feet, directly over the spot where the boil had last been seen. Moments later, shrugging and shaking itself from the depths like some befuddled whale, the ugly Russian submarine surfaced. The periscope climbed higher, natural buoyancy slicing it through the water as if the sub was actually under way. Then it sagged backward at a crazy angle, straightened, and thrust up to the sky at near perpendicular.

The sail surged up, followed almost instantly by the missile silos, then the decks and rails themselves. The sub's prow came up, settled back. Two or three sideways rolls, then it stabilized sluggishly.

The periscope was already rotating, a panic-stricken captain wild to see from which direction inevitable destruction would come. But he could not adjust the head to detect an enemy standing directly above.

Yak motioned the pilot into tighter position. The copter dropped until it was fifteen feet above the tower. "Ohara," Yak bellowed over the roar of the slapping rotors, "you know what you have to do."

Keio grinned, nodded, slid back the door. Without a moment's hesitation he went over the side, his foot groping for the pickup line stirrup, then hung from the line. At Katz's signal, the copilot dropped the line in three-foot steps.

Now Keio swung back and forth within three feet of the periscope head. He grabbed it with his left hand and dragged himself toward it. His .44 Auto-Mag appeared in his hand. Positioning himself three feet down on the shaft, Keio reached up and poked the barrel into the periscope's cowl. He ducked his head, then blew away the optics with one shot.

Keio chuckled as the copter swung over, playing out more line, dropping him onto the afterdeck.

The hoverbird dropped swiftly and hovered four feet above the deck until the Phoenix Force payload was dumped. As the pilot lifted off and stood by at thirty feet, he smiled amazedly at the pile of supplies on the sub's deck—a miniature beachhead!

Timing was critical. The Arabs were awaiting their attack; Phoenix's only advantage was to give it to them quicker and harder than they expected.

Thus each man deployed himself with swift precision, mechanically rehearsed in his assignment.

Keio swept up his Ingram MAC-10 (only using the Ingram for the close-quarter killing he knew was at hand) plus an explosives-jammed satchel, and then he raced for the sail. Clambering up the steel ladder as soundlessly as he was able, he then darted onto the bridge deck and began ladling six-inch thick skeins of plastic around the lip of the main hatch. He tamped the stuff down with firm yet delicate touch, forcing into every crevice.

By the time he had finished there was enough nitro ribboned around the hatch to turn an M48 medium tank on its back.

Keio finished by building a hump in the plastic and affixing detonator line. Then he deserted the sail cowling, began stealthily stringing wire down the deck, working toward the stern where a magneto waited.

Simultaneously Encizo and Manning had executed similar maneuvers, preparing the muzzle hatches leading down into the missile firing sections.

McCarter was working on an emergency escape hatch located halfway between the bow and the sail.

Katzenelenbogen unpacked additional grenades, scurried back and forth between team members, placing the grenades in handy line near each hatch as backup in case the initial half-dozen death-eggs failed to do their work.

The operation consumed four minutes.

Within the bowels of the Russian sub, utter confusion reigned.

"What do you mean, you can't see anything?" Ghazawi raged, dragging Commander Haddad away from the periscope, pushing his own swarthy face into the eye-cups.

"What did that *Jehudi* bastard do?" he seethed as his eyes met with nothing but gray watery light in the viewer.

He whirled, riveted Janda Yamani with the glittering stare of a fanatic. "You, send a party forward, protect the hatch there. We must cover every contingency should there be any attempt to blast open our seals."

"It is suicide," Yamani protested, for the first time contradicting his superior's orders. "We will all die."

"Suicide? You cowardly filth! Suicide for them!" screamed the unhinged Ghazawi. "We will be ready for them. The first enemy to show his face will get his head blown off!" He advanced threateningly on Yamani. "Or else you do...."

Yamani reluctantly commandeered a small task force while his Jeddah leader turned on another adjutant. "You, Fawzhir, go to the rear with six men. It will be your responsibility to see that the missile hatches are secure. We are especially vulnerable in that area!" He pointed violently at four remaining hardmen. "You will remain with me, and with Commander Haddad. We will protect the bridge area. They will expend their main force right here."

Again Ghazawi's eyes rolled wildly in his head. Then he turned his face upward, his gaze darting, as if he could see through the steel plate, could assess the action that must be taking place on the submarine's deck. He strained for any sounds of steel, any pound of boots, through the steel cocoon. But no betraying noises carried down. There was only the debilitating roar of the forgotten diesels as they continued recharging the storage cells, plus the cottony, insulating drone of the air-circulation systems.

"In the name of Allah," Ghazawi grated to nobody in particular. "If we only had that damned scope...if I could just see what is going on out there."

Another unexpected turnabout: Ghazawi noticed that Haddad's men, one by one, were slowly deserting their stations, were fading into the shadowy depths of the submarine. One moment a man would be at his post, the next the section would be totally deserted.

"What is this?" he roared at Haddad. "Your crew, what are they doing?" He caught one green-uniformed technician attempting to sidle out of sight. "You there! Stop where you are. Stop or I will kill you where you stand!" The man froze in place. "Haddad! Get your men back to their posts! That's an order!"

"They will not fight," Haddad whined, his voice flat, defeat shining in his gaze. "They are loyal to Pasha Khaddafi...they have no use for Jeddah...Jeddah has brought them to this accursed end."

"And you?" the wild Ghazawi challenged Haddad. "Will you flee also? Will you join your cowardly eunuchs?"

"I will stay," Haddad replied resolutely, but there was no real edge to his voice. "I will fight with you, my brother. I am an Arab to the last. I will die at your side." A zealot glaze filmed his eyes. "If I can take one last *Jehudi* swine with me when I go, I will have fulfilled Allah's destiny for me."

"I salute you, Commander," Ghazawi muttered. But the rage-fueled bravado choked as swiftly as it arose.

"Where are the *Amrikani*?" he groaned. "Why don't they attack?"

Terror and indecision compounded upon itself, and Ghazawi commenced to prowl the now-abandoned command area, his head tilted at extreme angle, searching for any new sound from above.

Finally his innate cowardice prevailed, and almost before he recognized the defection for what it was, he found himself crouched in a corridor leading aft, his terror an almost palpable thing. He was covering for the main force, he reassured himself. When, in all truth, he was thinking only of himself—he was covering his own greasy ass, nothing more.

But maybe it was the smartest thing the Jeddah head man had done that whole morning. Possibly the only smart thing the snivelling creature had done in a long, long time.

The charges detonated above. The horrendous concussion, the bone-compacting shock, tore through the compartments. The decks buckled and screeched.

Ghazawi was spared the full impact of the four-barreled explosion that ripped his cigar vessel. He was rocked, then flung against a bulkhead, but he was not flattened out unconscious on the floor as were the rest of the Jeddah forces.

Though his hands had instantly clamped to his ears, Ghazawi was not quick enough, he could not totally counteract the effect of the explosive hell that blasted the breath from his body. He felt a pop and tug inside his head, felt a sudden loss in his right ear—a shadowy, faint hissing suddenly ignited there—and knew he'd lost one eardrum.

As the demoralizing thunder rolled through the steel coffin, his terror magnified; he was crushed from without and within. There could be no escape from this hellish tinder box.

Even so, he drew up his U.S. Army M-16 and checked to see that the fresh clip was properly aligned in its seating. He was determined to fight to the death, because he wanted to take Katzenelenbogen with him. . . .

The resolve was hard to sustain, for as the sub ceased its stunning reverberations, as the smoke cleared the slightest bit, he saw Haddad, flung like a rag doll by the concussion, slowly sagging down a bulkhead, his face strangely disarranged by the blast, his eyes popped, gouts of blood pouring from his mouth and nose. Even as he watched, the brave man—more true to his code than Ghazawi had been—dropped to his knees, fell forward onto his face. He was dead before he hit the steel plating.

It was now that Ghazawi, for all his last-minute vainglorious bluster, reverted to type. His heart hammering crazily in his chest, his brain alive with a thousand confused shrieks of dismay, fear and confusion, the leader fell back on his position. Like some skulking dog, he sought the darkest shadows; he cowered deeper and deeper into the wet secret womb of the submarine.

The view from the top: finally all the detonating lines had been strung. Gathered aft, all lying prone, leeched to the wet deck slopes, Phoenix Force waited for Gary Manning, crouching on one knee above them, to jam the magneto plunger down. All hatches would be blown at the same time.

"Allow fifteen seconds," Yak briefed one last time. "Let the smoke die down. Then drop the MK 20 stuff, four sticks to a hatch. If eight pounds of composition C-3 doesn't blow the hatch itself, it'll sure as hell crack the scuttles."

He squinted against the sun, faint trace of a tremor in his voice. "After that we attack, use the hooks Next we pour grenades inside as fast as we can toss them. We crash the sail hatch and the forward emergency hatch simultaneously. Gary and Keio are forward—the rest of us take the sail area. Got it?"

"Got it," chorused four hushed voices.

Manning slammed the plunger down, hit the deck, clamped his hands to his ears, all in one movement.

Four mighty blasts tore the air, set up a stunning thunder, a massive concussive shock that emptied lungs, jolted bodies, made ears ring painfully even through cupped hands. They were lifted a foot off the plates, then slammed down with jolting force. Waves of compacted air literally shimmered before their eyes.

They caught glimpse of the sail hatch whizzing through the air over their heads, slicing into the ocean like a huge circular saw blade. One of the muzzle hatches stood at crazy angle, twisted in a blackened smoking warp.

"Now!" Yak barked. Phoenix Force lunged up, raced for their respective stations.

At each hatch, haversacks were deftly rifled, blocks of C-3 pressed into precise position in the inner trunk. Detonator line reels sang as each man returned to the magneto. Yak feverishly screwed down connections. Three minutes later—

"Gary!" Again the plunger dropped. Again the world exploded, rocking Phoenix Force anew.

There was no command this time. Sight of Yak loping forward, his hand clawing for grenades even as he ran, was all the signal they needed.

The sail tower was still smoking when Yak, Rafael and David reached it, but they ignored the smoldering steel and climbed up the shattered fairing at breakneck pace, Encizo picking up the steel hook on his way. Thick leather gloves already on, McCarter spun the quick acting scuttle, chuckled as he felt the latch give way. At the same time, Rafael was hooking onto the scuttle ring.

David helped him pull back the hundred-fifty-pound hatch. All ducked as a Jeddah opened up belowdecks, his M-16 on full automatic. Once his magazine was emptied, Katz began lobbing grenades down the hole as fast as he could pull and throw.

BLAMMO, BLAMMO, BLAMMO!

Nobody was shooting anymore.

And when the sixteenth grenade had tumbled into the Bedouin snake pit, when only muted screams and groans could be heard—

"Me first!" McCarter demanded, his full fury unleashed. "I get first chance at them fucking animals!"

Katz nodded resignedly. David vaulted over the cowling and paused briefly on the bridge deck to direct two bursts of 9mm parabellums down into the sub. With a yell, he hurtled down the ladder, using every fourth rung only, his Ingram chattering all the way. The last six feet was free-fall. He emptied his thirty-two round magazine, slapped in a fresh one, even as Encizo tumbled down beside him. Katz, not at all hampered by his steel claw, was close on Encizo's heels.

Inside the submarine, chaos. The murky compartments and passageways were choked up with eye-burning smoke. They could make out three mangled bodies—one in officer's braid—scattered about the bridge area. As their eyes adjusted to the gloom, they indiscriminately sprayed the maze of tanks, tubing and electrical cable with precautionary tumblers.

"Down!" Yak bellowed, whirling to drop an Arab behind Rafael and David. Ahmed's M-16 was blasted from his grasp, Yak's burst nearly decapitating him. The terrorist spun backward bounced off a bulkhead, died in a slide to the deck.

Suddenly Keio and Gary, who had stormed the forward hatch, popped into view forty feet down the line, flushing two more Jeddahs before them. "Hot stuff coming through!" Yak rasped. His muzzle flash turned the narrow passageway momentarily bright as day. Two more Arab hardmen headed for Allah-bye land, gushing blood like punctured ketchup containers.

"Clear?" Yak called.

"Clear between here and there," Keio responded. "We'll head to the torpedo room." Ohara and Gary wheeled, pouring a stream of hot lead ahead of them as they jogged.

Rafael, Katz and David advanced foot by wary foot down the corridor, flanked on both sides by an awesome aggregation of engineering. Seemingly a million miles of steam pipes, water pipes, hydraulic lines and electrical cable were wound up in this Rube Goldberg nightmare, jamming every square inch of ceiling and wall.

Cautiously they inched into the main part of the engine room, then saw a glistening trail of blood left by a wounded Jeddah. "Dumb bastards ain't minding their gauges and knobs," McCarter said. "How'n hell do they expect to get to Libya that way?"

The smoke was clearing, strong draft pushing through the sub from the savaged hatches. They could see better now; breathing became easier. For a moment they forgot caution, stood a little straighter.

An M-16 opened up, the slugs screaming inches above Rafael and Davey's head. Both hit the deck, slid in a puddle of blood. Yak fell back and sideways, barely avoiding the burst.

Yak's Ingram came up and spewed chewing lead to the spot where the Arab was tucked between two boilers. But the man was already on the move. Yak and David opened up a second time on the darting figure.

Their slugs tore open a steam-pressure tank behind the gunman. Jets of thousand-degree steam screamed from the boiler, caught the fleeing man in mid-stride.

He squealed like a stuck pig as the steam enveloped him broadside, its pressure spinning him to the deck. He struggled up insanely and staggered toward them, hands clamped to his face. Even as he drew his fingers away, sheets of skin came away with his fingers; his face, his hands were raw bloody meat. Scream after scream tore his throat. He fell again, crawled imploringly toward Enciso, his face a ghoulish mask, eyes awash with blood. Rafael mercifully put a bullet through his brain.

The trio surged forward, shooting ahead of them, fighting to see through the billowing steam.

Finally they groped their way through another access, escaping the main brunt of the steam. They saw a bright glare from an overhead connecting hatch.

"There are condensers up there," Yak reminded Enciso. "A lot of generators and inverters. You remember the layout. Take cover the minute you make it."

McCarter still running point, they came to within twenty feet of the connecting ladder when the Ghazawi bunch opened up, pouring bullets down the hole in manic, deadly rangabang.

All dropped, rolled. The slugs ricocheted crazily through the serpentine tangle of pipes, cables and equipment. Enciso felt a whining slug cleave the air six inches from his eyes.

Then: "Dirty, rotten bastards!" roared McCarter. "Nicked me!" He raised his head, and they saw blood welling along his right cheek.

"That's my good side, too," he seethed. "I'll get you for that, you buggers!" Rashly he darted up, skittered ten feet closer, unclipping grenades from his belt as he ran. "Here!" he howled. "A present from the bloody Queen."

They covered their heads as three grenades exploded. David gave them ten seconds. Then he charged up the ladder, his submachine gun fanning the entire maneuvering compartment.

Enciso saw David's feet dart right. Then he too

was up the ladder, hugging the floor, rolling left and firing at the same time. Rafael edged over, worked his way around the tall, ribbed condenser, making room for Katz as he flung himself down beside David.

The stun effect of the grenades fading among the survivors, the rapid-fire chatter of the M-16s took up again, peppering the decks and the walls in metallic clamor. A spent slug dropped in the folds of Rafael's trousers and burned him. He cursed.

"Hunak," a tall, thin Arab called out. "Over there. Get them! Kill the *Jehudi*!"

A shame, Encizo thought, getting the man in his sights from the far side of the condenser. I would have liked doing it slow—hand-to-hand—I'd take your skin off by inches. Savoring the moment, he lovingly wrapped his finger on the trigger, depressed it that last millimeter. The Ingram barked twice, obliterating the man's face, painting the bulkhead behind him with brain vomit.

Janda Yamani did not suffer as much as Phoenix might have wished, had they known who he was, and the part he had played in the ugly Red Bluff massacre. They would have devised hellish tortures for the bastard. But he suffered hardly at all.

Even in death, however, he was still one vicious *hombre*. For as Yamani fell—his weapon stupidly set on automatic, his finger still in the M-16's trigger ring—he wiped out a fellow hardman at his side.

His buddy released an incredulous scream, fell flopping, grossly gut-wounded, onto the deck, where he oozed his entrails into his hands.

The bloody demonstration served good purpose.

For immediately the four men who were cowering in the compartment bolted, heading for safer climes. Idiotically they abandoned cover, started for a doorway leading into the missile compartment.

Saturday night at the county fair. Except that these weren't puny .22s stitching them to the wall. These were the real McCoy.

Three men piled up, made a particularly bloody doormat. The fourth man miraculously escaped a hit, somehow clawed his way over the top of the life-oozing heap of ex-humanity.

He chose to avenge his fallen comrades. His rifle swung up. His psychotic eyes sought a target.

Three Ingrams opened up simultaneously.

The would-be hero need never have to worry about dandruff again. The top of his head was, all at once, not there anymore.

For long moments the trio panned with their Ingrams, ready for any last surprise that might still crawl out of the ironwork. Finally, when relative calm closed down—last dying moans, the drip-drip of blood the only sound to be heard—Phoenix Force exhaled a unanimous sigh of relief.

The sweet cloying stench of death was everywhere. In hurried inventory, McCarter counted eight bodies—six fresh kills, plus two mangled grenade victims just inside the hatch. He grimaced as his feet slipped in a congealing glaze of blood.

"Christ, what a mess," he muttered. "It'll cost our friend Khaddafi a mint to put this place back to rights."

"Not to worry," Encizo joined in. "Congress will lend him the money. At one percent."

"How many more do you think there are?" David asked.

"Hard to tell," Yak replied. "What puzzles me is the crew. Where are they? They'd be dressed in green uniforms. It's madman Khaddafi's favorite color. So far, just one green outfit...the captain...when we first came down."

Encizo kicked over a body. "Is this Ghazawi?"

"No. He's not ugly enough. I expect he's in the torpedo room. I guess it's too much to expect that Gary or Keio will leave me a bit of that action." Yak sighed. "Pity."

He looked with concern at McCarter, who was staunching the flow of blood from his cheek with a handkerchief. "How bad is it, Davey? Let's take a look."

"Nothing at all, Yak," he said. "A war souvenir. Another scar to enhance my dashing good looks. It turns the ladies on."

"Good looks?" Encizo gibed good-naturedly. "The only thing that'll help that face is a direct hit."

"There you go, mate," Davey laughed. "That's calling 'em like you see 'em. Only in your case it wouldn't help at all, you poor homely greaseball."

Forward, just outside the torpedo room, Manning and Ohara faced a standoff.

There was no way of appraising enemy strength within; the hatch had just been slammed, the scuttle spinning mockingly in their faces. A solid clunk on the bolt, and they were locked in for the winter.

"Only one thing to do," Manning said. "Blow the hatch."

"Why not wait them out? They aren't going any-where."

"Blood's what it's all about, Keio. And they named the game. I want my share," said the usually stolid ex-mining engineer.

Within seconds, Manning had a block of C-3, a coil of fuse, a manual igniter in his hands. "Now, let's see," he mused, taping the explosive to the scuttle housing. "If the concussion doesn't get them, we sure as hell will."

In seconds more, detonator pre-imbedded, the medium-light charge was ready. Keio swiftly played out six feet of fuse.

Manning hurried to the far end of the gloomy chamber and called up to the men in the maneuvering compartment. "We're gonna blow a hatch, gang. Brace yourselves."

Then he raced back, hit the igniter. The fuse hissed happily, easing its deadly little fireball toward the hatch at a leisurely few seconds per foot.

Gary and Keio calmly retreated, went to the hatch opening, clambered onto the deck. "Ten seconds," he roared back into the hole at the last. "Keep those mouths open!"

He and Keio braced themselves against the sail fairing and covered their ears. The sub suddenly shuddered beneath their feet, the concussion jarring ankle and knee joints, a bluish-white flareback leaping from the hatch opening. Both men wondered what the impact had done to those inside the torpedo room—caught by total surprise, locked in their ten-by-twenty-foot steel cave....

Swiftly they rose, tumbled back inside, the smoke

stench gagging them. Now they charged down the long corridor, their feet clanging steel. The Ingrams came up, ready for bloody *coup de grace*.

The hatch door had blown inward, and now it sagged on its warped hinges. A ring of fire ate at the rubber insulating ring.

There was no need for caution. There would be no resistance from the three torpedo-room holdouts today.

One son of hell had taken the full brunt of the explosion and lay on the deck behind the still-smoldering hatch. Apparently near the door when the charge went off, he was the victim of a completely crushed skull. He had obviously hit the steel bulkhead behind him full force, the impact disintegrating every bone in his body. His cranium was flattened like a ripe squash, turned to a muddied chowder of blood, bone and flesh.

The second Jeddah hardman stood in blind confusion in the compartment's center, blood pouring from his mouth and ears and eyes. He walked in tight circles, aimless, his hands groping. Low hysterical Arabic gibberish came from his cherry-red mouth.

Now it was Keio's turn to put a man out of misery. He directed a burst into the Arab's heart and blasted him backward against a rack of torpedoes.

The third man was in final throes of death also. The concussion had shot him backward, launching him horizontally, jamming his head and shoulders into one of the gaping torpedo tubes all the way to his elbows. Instant vacuum had been formed, and he was, even now, being suffocated. His feet kicked feebly a half dozen times, finally went still.

"Manning? Ohara?" Yak called from behind them.

"Okay here," Gary said. "They're taken care of. The blast did it." He made a face. "Rum show."

McCarter squeezed past, glanced into the compartment. "Holy Mary and all the saints," he gasped. "I guess so. Now I've seen everything."

As the weary, dirty, bloodstained marauders crouched in the narrow passageway to get their second wind, an uncanny silence settled inside the claustrophobic shell. A deceiving sense of finality and peace descended upon them.

But they were not done yet.

Enzico broke the morbid impasse: "Ghazawi?" he addressed Yak. "He in there?"

"No," Yak answered. "Those ones are too small. Ghazawi's a gross tub of human shit."

"Where is he then?" Keio said.

"Ready for more hide and seek?" sighed Yak.

All arose, made united show of adjusting cartridge belts, reloading, rearranging grenades on their webbing.

16

Single file, with Yak leading, they proceeded to the sail area. They located the hatch that led down to the second level. Again they paused, strained to hear movement belowdecks. Nothing.

Decisively Yak scuttled down the metal rungs. He froze partway down, eyes darting, expecting the stuttering snarl of an M-16 at any moment. Three more steps. A sweeping gesture with the Ingram. Still nothing.

He dropped the last four feet to the deck, loped to the left. Encizo and Manning dropped beside him, while McCarter and Ohara brought up the rear, deployed to the opposite corridor.

"A'rabee kalbi!" Yak yelled down the echoing passageway. "Arab dogs! Do you come out to fight, or do you hide like the turd-sniffing cowards you are?"

For emphasis he sent a short burst of 9mm slugs to the farthest end of the corridor. "Fight, you women!"

Abruptly, as the echoes died down, a muffled murmuring, a chantlike wail carried from behind the closed doors.

"They're praying," Yak said in astonishment. "The bastards are reciting the Koran."

Then, down the hall, a door floated halfway open. Yak motioned his crew to hold its fire. *"Effendi,"* the muted, disembodied voice carried, *"effendi,* don't shoot."

"Who speaks?" he continued in Arabic. "What are your terms?"

"Full surrender," the voice pleaded. "We are not armed. We are only poor sailors. We do not want to die."

"The crew," Yak translated, "they want to surrender." Then down the line: "Show yourself!"

The door swung wider, and a white towel tied to a stick was thrust out. A moment later, a green-uniformed officer, obviously second-in-command, appeared with terrified expression.

He inched forward, his eyes on Yak's submachine gun. "We are not members of Jeddah," he said, "we did not ask for this mission. Pasha Khaddafi ordered us to take these bandits off that accursed American ship. We wish to surrender. Spare our lives, *effendi.*"

Speaking rapidly, Yak accepted their surrender, ordered the officer to muster his crew.

Commands rang out; the officer went down the passageway banging on doors. The sub's complement—twenty-four in all—emptied into the corridor.

"Check those quarters for hidden arms," Yak barked.

Minutes later David and Gary returned. "Clean, Yak," Gary reported. "No sign of any weapons."

"Where is Khader Ghazawi?" Yak demanded.

"He is not with us," the XO responded. "He was on the command deck with Captain Haddad when all the explosions started. We all fled here.'' His eyes rolled, amazed that just five men had wreaked all this destruction. "Please, Commander, do not kill us too...."

The officer was to restrict his men to quarters; they were not to budge until they received further orders. Understood?

The Arab nodded abjectly. A moment later his babbling crew began crowding back into their quarters.

"Manning. You and Encizo have had quite a day already. Stay here, guard these guys," said Katz.

"C'mon, Yak," Rafael pleaded, "don't give us this flunky detail. We want to be in on the finish."

"We've got all the help we need, Encizo." Katz sent a rueful grin.

Manning too walked down the corridor to station himself outside the last door.

"You," Yak addressed the Arab XO, "come along with us."

The man went pale, started to protest. Then, thinking better of it, he meekly fell into place behind Katzenelenbogen. They started back up the ladder.

Minutes were wasted in the forward tunnels and compartments. Two grenades were thrown, a dozen rounds of ammo expended.

But Ghazawi was not flushed.

Next they worked their way back toward the sail area, skulking through the lower levels, their heels clanging hollowly in the vast steel maze.

It was as they reinvaded the command area, struck forward to the missile compartments, that Ghazawi tipped his hand. Determined to take infidel souls with him as he died, he foolishly committed himself too soon.

In the fury of the first Phoenix charge through the command area, he had hoisted himself out through one of the missile hatches, thus deserting forever his fellow terrorists.

It was McCarter who caught sight of the flitting shadow. He saw it across the right hand hatch as they headed forward. His reaction was pure reflex. "Down!"

Instantly the command room exploded as a deafening dozen M-16 rounds smashed down the hatch, were deflected off the deck, caromed upward at a thirty-five-degree angle to ricochet among the convoluted tangle of pipes and cables and ducts overhead. The targeted avengers froze, doubled over, as slugs shrieked a foot above their heads.

Except for McCarter, who opened up with his Ingram even as he dropped and rolled. His tumblers poured out of the opening in deadly stream, brushed the coward back.

Ghazawi dropped, had to crawl along the deck until he reached cover in the fairing just behind and below the sail structure.

It was a fool's move. For there was, in fact, no cover. He was a scuttling rat caught on a steel prairie, a thousand miles of nothingness on all sides of him.

"Up!" rasped Yak. "Get him!"

David started up the twenty-foot ladder that led to the tower's flying bridge. Yak followed close on his heels.

Keio raced for the forward hatch and flung himself

at the ladder there. His submachine gun, seeming extension of his arm, ached for Ghazawi to show his face in the gaping hole above.

The terror XO had furtively slunk into the shadows, wedging himself under a control canopy until all this killing would be done with.

Then, hearing the clatter, feeling the vibrations through the steel, Ghazawi abandoned his hiding place. Flopping on his belly, he made for the protective curvature of a missile silo.

In panic now, he was torn by a dozen conflicting passions. Should he die fighting? Should he bargain, try to save his skin? Should he pray to the white people's devil for a miracle of deception that would take the *Jehudi* bastard to death with him?

He saw McCarter cautiously poke his head from the tower and duck back. A last leap around the end of the tube and he was ready. Wedged in the swale between the missile silos, Ghazawi waited for the *Amrikani* to show his face again.

His M-16 chattered savagely as David appeared a second time. But his cramped position threw him off. The slugs hit low, spattering the steel plate two feet below his enemy's face.

McCarter drew back, shook his head to clear the painful clanging in his ears, cursed vehemently.

Then there was return fire as Keio came topside, slithering around the fairing, finding his footing, darting up to trigger a quick burst at the Arab. The 9mm slugs caromed off the silo, screamed off into the blue, set up booming echo in the cylinders. Paint scales puffed up that momentarily blinded Ghazawi, further disorienting him.

He wheeled, spraying the spot where Keio had been. Again there was movement in the tower, and he swung his muzzle over, directed a fresh burst to keep McCarter down. Terror mounted. All this was happening too fast. He was not equipped, never had been, to cope with this kind of confusion.

For terrorists operated under the cover of darkness. Terrorists planted bombs, killed innocent women and children, unsuspecting athletes and tourists. Terrorists shot down drugged sleepwalking troops in cold blood. Terrorists never confronted the enemy face-to-face. And certainly not in broad daylight, naked to their enemies.

Heart-hollowing fear grew, and as he waited for the next frontal assault he wished that some of the men he had so cravenly deserted could be here with him. If he had help, then he could be brave. But they were gone, and his aloneness was a crushing thing.

Now Ghazawi was embarrassed as he found his bladder had betrayed him. Hot piss cascaded down his leg, soiled his fatigues. His groan of disgust verged on humiliating tears.

There, in the tower! Here was his chance! He clamped the trigger, sent ten more rounds toward the despised infidel. But the bullets screamed harmlessly into empty space. Ghazawi whirled, shot at the fairing to keep the other one down.

He cursed, knew momentary paralysis. The stupid American rifle was jammed! Then he realized it was not jammed; the magazine was empty. But there was no time to reload. They would be upon him at any moment. Once they realized his helpless position—

His mental circuits totally blitzed, he went amok.

Keio's head popped up on the far side of the silos. He saw Ghazawi shaking forty feet away, fighting the M-16, dancing in madness, his visible body bathed in sweat.

Hope of taking the Jeddah leader alive for Yak crossing Keio's mind, he reacted reflexively. Letting his Ingram droop on its strap, he yanked his .44 AutoMag from his belt and slapped off the safety He took careful aim.

The first shot was for range, the second for effect. The thunderball slug splintered the M-16's flimsy stock, ripped the weapon from the Arab's grasp. Ghazawi grunted with pain, watched dazedly as the gun spun across the deck to slide down the slope and drop into the ocean.

Ghazawi stood in schizophrenic trance, his face distorted with indecision. He fought to suppress a womanish scream, final sense of unreality sweeping over him. The dark stain in his trousers grew still larger.

"Don't move, creep," Keio snarled.

David's head popped over the lip of the shattered tower cowling. Then Yak's. "Hold him right there, Keio," Yak called down. "We're on our way."

Even as Katzenelenbogen advanced on the cowering Arab hardman, handing his Ingram to Keio as he came, all three knew what would happen next. This was a personal vendetta here. Ghazawi had cursed the memory of Yak's dead son; he had gloated over the death of a brave Israeli patriot.

"No, no..." Ghazawi blubbered. He read only too clearly the insane fury in his enemy's eyes. "Spare me, I beg you...."

Yakov wasted no time with words. His fist, his feet, the steel claw on his right arm, all churned with blurred action. A kick to the fat slug's groin, a knee to his chin as, screaming, he hunched over to protect his shattered balls.

A second later there was further reason to scream. Yak's twin hooks on the end of his right arm slashed through the terror leader's left cheek, puncturing the flesh, twisting and hooking, tearing a flap of skin away, leaving a gaping hole.

Again the hook descended, this time destroying the Arab's left ear.

Ghazawi despairingly flung himself at Yak, clinching, fighting for time. If he could just regain his scorched senses enough to retrieve the Walther PPK concealed in his clothes—

"Yak, watch out!" Keio warned. "He's got a knife!"

Ohara flung himself forward even as the Arab hardman dragged the stubby AKM bayonet from an improvised scabbard on Yak's belt, the man smiling bemusedly through his pain, astonished at his lucky find.

Yak reacted swiftly, twisted under the slashing arm, and whirled away from Ghazawi. But the Arab, infused with a paranoid bravado, hung on, raising the knife a second time. He slashed down.

Keio intervened, beating David to it by a single step. Even so, burdened with Yak's Ingram as well as his own, Keio was awkward, off-balance. His right hand closed on Ghazawi's shoulder, grabbed a piece of uniform, half turned him.

Yak had finished his fall-away and gave Ghazawi a

last shove. Suddenly the Arab hardman became medieval in his wild flailings. The combination of opposing thrusts gave his knife arm an extra iota of speed and force.

Keio's eyes went wide with disbelief as the blade sank into his chest, dug through his diaphragm, just at the terminus of his rib cage.

Keio was as amazed at his own failure to ward off the blow as he was at the gravity of his wound.

He moaned softly, wound his fingers around the bayonet handle, sank slowly to the deck.

Yak went crazy. Viciously he wrenched his Ingram up from the deck where it had fallen. His face contorted with rage—rage at Ghazawi, rage at himself for wallowing in callow vendetta that exposed his comrades to risk—he opened up at point-blank range. The trigger on full automatic, he emptied what remained of the magazine—twelve rounds— into Ghazawi. The impact straightened the victim, sent shredded chunks of flesh flying into the air behind him. He was driven back a full five feet on the deck. His feet went out from under him and he canted over the chain rail, rolled down the hull incline into the ocean, his slide leaving a gory streak on the plates.

As Ghazawi floated lifelessly in the water, Yak jammed another magazine into the Ingram. His face a diabolic mask, he emptied the entire thirty-two rounds into the bobbing corpse. He methodically sprayed the terrorist from head to hips, then back again.

The water turned red around Ghazawi, a dark, floating marine cloud that widened by the second. At long last the obscenely riddled carcass had the decency to sink into the ocean.

Keio had made move to withdraw the knife, but Yak forestalled him. "Leave it. There's a saw edge. We'll have help, expert help, for you within minutes."

Ashen-faced, McCarter waved the hovering copter down.

As they carefully arranged Keio on the copter deck and Yak climbed aboard: "Hang tough, Davey," he ordered. "Tell the others what came off. We'll take Keio to the *Nimitz*. They've got doctors, equipment there. If anyone can pull him through, they can."

The chopper lifted off. "I'll have a cleanup crew back shortly," he called down. And to the pilot: "Get the *Nimitz* on the radio. Alert them for badly wounded...."

17

The men of Phoenix Force were gathered around Keio's bed in the *Nimitz* infirmary. Self-conscious, excessively hearty to conceal deep concern and affection for their buddy, they had gathered for short-term farewells. All knew they would be together again soon—sooner than they liked, should truth be known.

Yak, Rafael, David and Gary would be airborne within the half-hour. A Grumman Tracker would deposit them in Norfolk by nightfall. From there they would be shuttled to Stony Man Farm for final wrapup. Two days of debriefing and brain picking, and each member of John Phoenix's American foreign legion would once more sink back into his particular piece of the woodwork, resume the normal patterns of his life.

If the word normal could, in any way, be used to describe this rugged, this iconoclastic, this determined breed of men.

"I envy you, Keio," McCarter smiled down at the wan-faced Oriental, "getting to hang around here. All that good grub. Pretty nurses. That blonde who just went by—did you see the hub caps on that?"

"Here we go again," Keio murmured weakly. "Talk about one-track minds."

Two days had passed. Two hectic, anxiety-crammed days. And only yesterday afternoon, late, the welcome news had come: Keio was beyond danger. But only quick transfer to the *Nimitz* and the cool efforts of a crack surgical team had stood between him and the grim reaper.

"No work with weights for a while, my friend," Yak said, voice tingled with emotion, gratitude foremost in his thoughts. "We promise you'll get in on the next mission. We wouldn't be a team without you, you know that."

"Fuckin' A," Davey agreed.

The Dessler Laser Submachine Guns had been recovered, all in mint condition; also the prototype mortars seized during the murderous Red Anvil raid. The Arab crew had been transferred, were now stashed in the *Nimitz* brig, awaiting word from State as to what would be done with them.

Body count on Jeddah hardmen had been made; it was assumed every last one had been killed. Should any still be hiding in some secret cranny aboard the submarine, it was of no consequence. A naval demolition team had gone aboard yesterday, put her to the bottom for good.

The entire matter was classified. All military personnel had been ruthlessly strong-armed into secrecy; no word of the caper would ever find its way into the national or international press.

Perhaps one day the world would learn how close it had come to a Middle Eastern blowup. One day the exploits of a phantom fighting force might become public knowledge. But for now—

Phoenix Force? A myth, nothing more.

Khaddafi would shake himself soon from his megalomaniac stupor and realize he hadn't heard from Jeddah or Red Anvil in quite some time. And whatever happened to that submarine he had dispatched some months back?

And where to direct polite inquiry?

Not to the U.S. State Department, certainly.

"Luck, *compadre*," Rafael said gruffly, shaking Keio's hand a bit longer than was necessary. "Take care, and all that shit. Catch you next trip. Maybe we'll win an easy one next time—standing guard on a feather factory or some such."

One by one they came up, exchanged curt, bantering goodbyes.

"Glad you made it, Keio," Manning joshed, a special earnestness in his smile. "You're a good sidekick. Sure would hate to lose you. Be a pain in the ass breaking in a new man."

They all paused in the doorway, waved back down the ward. A nurse edged past them toward Keio. Even from a distance, the Japanese hero saw McCarter pantomime a double grab at her bouncy pneumatic ass.

But it sure hurt him to laugh.

FR STONYMAN ONE STONYMAN OPS
TO BROGNOLA WASHDC

GREAT VICTORY BY PHOENIX FIVE OVER LETHAL
JEDDAH CONSPIRACY X CONVEY TO LEADER THIS
MISSION KATZ THAT SUCCESSFUL ACTION IS FRESH
START FOR PHOENIX FORCE X DESSLER SLG
PROTOTYPES VITAL TO WESTERN INTERESTS AND
YOU SHOULD KNOW TOPMAN AMERICA ONE IS
PASSIONATELY AWARE OF PHOENIX FORCE TRIUMPH
X ONLY CONCERN THAT KO JOINS ABLE CL AS
WOUNDED IN ACTION X THEIR BLOOD IS MY BLOOD X
RAGE IS CONTROLLED BUT THERE AS EVER X ALL
NOW KEEP COOL THATS OFFICIAL X DEEP GRATITUDE
AND ADMIRATION X WILL JOIN PF SOON X END
PERSBRIEF WRAPUP
BT
EOM

Mack Bolan's

PHOENIX FORCE

Somewhere in the world, terrorists strike. Innocent men and women are kidnapped and held hostage.

Then in cities scattered across the globe—Tel Aviv and Toronto, Tokyo, London and Miami—five very special men answer their telephones.

A voice speaks from a place called Stony Man Farm. It is terse and direct.

These men now have their mission: save hostages, destroy terrorists, wipe out organizations. Phoenix Force is in action once again.

The voice that speaks from Stony Man Farm belongs to Colonel John Phoenix, a.k.a. Mack Bolan, Mack the Bastard, The Executioner. The five men are the nucleus of his Phoenix Force, the United States' and the free world's secret weapon against the scourge of international terrorism. Their mandate: to go into action whenever and wherever terrorists unleash their cowardly war. It is a mandate to save civilization from the greatest danger it has confronted in centuries.

Few leaders could command the loyalty of these five fighters, but there are few men made like Colonel John Phoenix. Born Mack Bolan, for personal reasons he waged a one-man war of revenge against organized crime. The best efforts of the mafia and law-enforcement agencies could not stop him. He single-handedly eradicated evil men from the face of urban America in situations where the police and the courts had failed. At last the American government realized that Mack Bolan was a man who would not be beaten. They enlisted him in the struggle against terrorism. Bolan was seen to have died in fiery immolation in New York. Colonel John Phoenix arose from the ashes of that fire. With a new identity and the backing of the American government, Mack Bolan the Executioner became Colonel John Phoenix, and began building his Phoenix Force and his Able Team from a private stronghold at Stony Man Farm.

For fifteen years, the rise of international terrorism has ravaged the lives of innocent men, women and children in over 8,000 incidents of bombings, hijackings, kidnappings. Colonel Phoenix recognized that this was not a declared war of nations and armies. It was a war in which the enemy did not even dare to stand up and fight in the open, in which terrorists skulked through the cities of the world cowering behind civilians, disappearing into distant and inhospitable countryside.

Someone had to stop this terror whatever the personal cost, however far outside the law was the scope of the operation. Colonel John Phoenix was going to be that man. And however much killing or hatred his chosen goal involved, coming from Colonel Phoenix it sprang from his compassion for innocent victims of war, from a deep love for his country, and from his commitment to a universal ethic that calls for a never-ending war of attrition and containment to maintain the existence of life itself.

For the job ahead, Colonel Phoenix had to find the best, the men who could be trusted for their brains, their strength, their courage and their dedication. Loyal men who could be sent into hostile and stinking territory, who did not care about horrific conditions and totally unpredictable circumstances that were unbounded by any political controls. Men who embraced the opportunity to take risks. Men who did not expect to die in bed.

Free world intelligence computers spat out the names of six thousand candidates. Six hundred of these men were chosen for scrupulous performance and psychological testing. The sixty who scored highest were given personal interviews. Five men were chosen. Not for their competitive rating, but for their uniqueness.

Yak, or Yakov Katzenelenbogen, often known as Katz, was drawn from the ranks of the Mossad—the Israeli Intelligence Service. Yak is the senior member of Phoenix Force and has the experience to prove it. He started his career as a French-born boy in Palestine during the Second World War delivering bombs for the Stern Gang in his paperbag. Yak is a master of disguise, and none is more misleading than his usual appearance. He has one arm missing, blown off by an anti-personnel mine in the Five Day War, and he walks somewhat stiffly, sometimes with a cane. But cross his path and this one-armed man is a lethal blur of movement and action, his cane or his prosthetic arm becoming any one of several variations of a deadly weapon. Few survive with their lives intact.

Gary Manning, a rugged and calm-natured Canadian, started out as a civil engineer with a background in heavy construction and explosives. One day the FLQ stole a truckload of dynamite from his company. The RCMP wasn't much help, so Manning had to get it back. By himself. He succeeded. Although never formally trained for military assignments, Manning can handle a grenade like a cueball in a billiard game, and the inventive genius of Stony Man Farm supplies him with a variety of armaments, which his enemies invariably find most surprising.

Rafael Encizo works as a marine insurance investigator in Miami. He knows about ships and boats—and underwater demolition. A Cuban patriot, Encizo was captured during the ill-fated Bay of Pigs invasion. He was one of the strong ones. He survived the cells of Principe Prison. Betrayed by the powers-that-be at the Bay of Pigs, Encizo does not trust authority easily. But he figured that Colonel John Phoenix warranted his confidence. Encizo discovered that Phoenix, like himself, believed in justice—whatever laws had to be transcended to get it.

David McCarter was recruited from the British SAS as a commando veteran. He can also fly anything with a propeller and wings. His easygoing manner belies a suspicious nature and a temper with a short fuse. McCarter has a reputation as a cynic—the kind of cynic who lives for danger. He likes to thumb his nose at fate, figures life is not much worth living if a guy doesn't take a chance every now and again.

McCarter took a chance when he went into the Iranian Embassy in London to save hostages. The terrorists lost.

Death comes silently, and is very very swift when it comes in the form of Keio Ohara, the youngest member of Phoenix Force. KO, as in knock-out, as he was affectionately nicknamed by the other members of Phoenix Force, is a six-foot-tall Japanese para-commando and intelligence man with a background in electrical engineering and a handy specialization in communications equipment. He can whip up telephone scramblers faster than someone else can dial a number. But his best weapons are his hands. KO was trained in the death-dealing techniques of the martial arts.

The base center of operation for Phoenix Force is Stony Man Farm, Colonel John Phoenix's headquarters in the eastern U.S. and a complete military support system independent of the Pentagon. Underground bunkers and camouflaged installations provide training facilities and a supply network for guns, ammunition, data, currency, passports, identities, even support troops. Phoenix Force remains constantly in touch with Stony Man via a secret military satellite channel.

Put the five men of Phoenix Force together in the war room at Stony Man Farm and despite the wide divergence of nationality and appearance, they have one physical aspect in common—a look of keen alertness glinting in their eyes. These are men who miss nothing, who share the kind of camaraderie that comes only when fighting men depend on each other for their lives. They began in uncertainty—in Mack

Bolan's view in disadvantage and lost opportunity—
but by the time they pursued the Libyan Jeddah
enemy with a relentless hunger for action, they were
most decidedly on track. Deadly track.

Yakov, Manning, Encizo, McCarter and KO....
Each of them had a speciality to offer Phoenix Force,
just as each of them had his own reason for joining.
But when Colonel John Phoenix calls them, they no
longer have a past, or an identity. They are soldiers,
fighting in secret. There will be no reward or fame
for winning the battles of their covert war against terrorism.

While these five men serve Phoenix Force and the
interests of free world nations with unyielding loyalty, they also serve a higher master—justice in its
truest sense. To fight for justice is to give something
to the world. However secret that fight might be, in
the jungles of South America, the deserts of the Middle East, or in the urban landscapes of Europe's and
America's great cities, or under the sea, it makes the
men of Phoenix Force heroes of the most individual
and yet most selfless kind. Action and success!

ABLE TEAM

AN EXECUTIONER SERIES

#4 Amazon Slaughter

MORE ADVENTURE
COMING SOON!

Chin Pok was death incarnate. He had chosen the hunters of his private army very carefully—they were some of the most vicious hoodlums in the world.

Now he had his own plutonium factory, protected by a web of organized intrigue. There was only one way to take out Chin Pok and prevent global tragedy: Mack Bolan's Able Team!

To neutralize Pok's ghoulish scheme, Lyons, Schwarz and Blancanales probe to the core of the maniac's domain in South America—only to find blameless native slaves. Will there be a massacre of innocents before the despot could be sent to his doom?

Watch for new Able Team titles
wherever paperbacks are sold